Brandon Originals

All there is
Jennifer Cornell

Born in the USA of Irish and Italian descent, Jennifer Cornell spent much of the 1980s in the North of Ireland, working in a cross-community project in Belfast, and later took an MA in Peace Studies at the University of Ulster, Magee College. She returned to the USA to complete an MFA in Creative Writing at Cornell University before joining the English Dept. at Oregon State University where she now teaches creative writing.

Her short stories have been widely published on both sides of the Atlantic and have received several prizes and awards: this, her first collection, was awarded the Drue Heinz Literature Prize in 1994. The *New York Times* comments: 'Ms Cornell writes with a burnished melancholy and a soft wit, rolling out an undulating series of elegant images' in stories which are 'lucid, inventive and teeming with overlapping memories, like creamier versions of William Trevor's wry fables...'. Jennifer Cornell is currently working on a second collection of short stories, and is completing a non-fiction book on the representation of Northern Ireland in contemporary British television drama.

Published in 1995 by
Brandon Book Publishers Ltd
Dingle, Co. Kerry, Ireland

Copyright © Jennifer Cornell 1995

British Library Cataloguing-in-Publication Data is available for this book.

ISBN 0 86322 209 9

This book is published with the assistance of the Arts Council/
An Chomhairle Ealaion, Ireland.

First published as *Departures* by the University of Pittsburg Press, 1995.
This paperback edition published by arrangement with the University of
Pittsburgh Press.

Cover design by The Public Communications Centre Ltd, Dublin
Typeset by Koinonia, Bury
Printed by ColourBooks Ltd, Dublin

Contents

Heat

———

S HE LOOKS LIKE a young one, my father told me, while I was still too far behind him to see him. Careful now, he said, try not to frighten her. She was smaller than I had expected, and more fragile. Among the chestnut hairs that cloaked her back and shoulders there were longer, thicker strands of black, yet they too had an unexpected softness, and when the light breeze from the hills above the gully blew over her from behind, the smoky down of her inner coat stirred like a living thing against her skin. Be very quiet, my father said softly, but already her ears lay flat against her skull and her thin lids were drawn so tightly away from her eyes that the jaundiced whites jumped and flashed each time a sudden noise startled her into movement.

She was the first thing we'd captured since we started setting traps six weeks before. My father'd told me what Albert Freel had said, that April was too early, that animals grew sluggish in the summer heat and it was foolish to stalk them while they were still lean and wary with the memory of winter. Albert Freel had a stable of greyhounds, every one the colour of foam in the harbour at Larne, and when he walked them all together up the Shankill to the Woodvale Park he moved in the midst of a small, private sea. The false spring had tricked us, Albert said; five days of warm winds and sunshine and half the dogwoods in the cemetery had begun to bloom, and on the edges of tarmac all over the city bold blades of grass had suddenly appeared. Then the cold had unfolded with the weight of wet fabric, and those who'd been counting on the coming of summer barely had time to get out of the way.

The corridors of the traps we used were long and narrow;

collapsible doors at either end sprang up when unsettled and shut the unsuspecting in. Sheets of metal covered the inner mesh frames, all four panels made for removal: captives could be viewed that way without risking release. The plates slid in their grooves with the sound of knives being readied, yet every morning when we went to check them the doors of the traps had snapped shut on nothing, or else were still lying open, though the bait inside was gone.

This is how we came to set them. My father had been fixing the floor of a barn when a nest fell down from above straight into his arms. He'd held out his hands when he'd seen it coming, and then there they were: a trio of fledglings, still blind, open-mouthed, psoriatic with first plumage and the eczema of recent birth. A man from Ardoyne had been on the job with him; hearing the whistle of small things in motion, he'd practically bolted when he'd seen my father with a dry puff of dust rising up from his palms. The man's wife had had triplets and he needed the work – he'd spent three weeks fitting windows in Ballysillan, ten days in east Belfast on a decorating job, his wife had been sick with the worry of it but he'd kept his head down and his mind on the wage – but he was growing convinced that his luck was finished, and he'd taken the nest falling as some sort of sign. Just get rid of them, for chrissake, he'd argued, they're done for now, sure, anyway. But my father was thinking of a goldfinch he'd bought when he was first married, how the smell of fresh linen had made the bird sing whenever my mother brought clothes in from the line. So he'd shaken the rubble from his cap and whiskers, nestled the birdlings in an old canvas sack, and brought them back home as a present for me.

The first evening we had them we boiled porridge and my father tried to feed them with a kitchen spoon. They opened wide when their lips touched silver, but the cartilage kept catching on the spoon's heavy basin, and the hard, yellow corners of their mouths pulled away. So he made up a potion of egg yolk and mince, a few drops of milk, a bit of sugar, and with the aid of an eyedropper squeezed the pulp in. He fed them steadily till their hunger subsided and their heads started to loll, nodding in time with their impatient breathing and their shoulders shuddering in somnambulant flight. Well, wee woman, my father said finally, covering the box he'd found for them with a bit of muslin secured with twine, that'll be your job from now on.

They died on a Saturday about a week later while we were out shopping down in the town. There was a disturbance in the Castle Court complex – a suspect parcel had been found on a bench – and to pass the time we'd gone to Bewley's, where hundreds and thousands roll out from under whenever a teacup or platter is lifted, where even the dust is finely ground coffee and whatever's left over when chocolate is shaved. But after an hour my father decided that the purchase he'd forgotten in one of the dressing rooms when the security officers had asked us to leave was unlikely to be there when we were let back inside; so we paid our bill and headed back up the Shankill, through a thickness of people in optimistic attire – bright coloured jerseys and unbuttoned anoraks, a few boys in T-shirts, a few girls in shorts – all moving with the rustling sound of large, leafy vegetables packed upright in bags. Crossing Berlin Street we heard the explosion. Wouldn't you know it, my father said, turning back towards the city to look for the smoke. We could have just waited; it's all over now.

The shock must have shaken the legs of the table, for the box lay on its side on the floor when we got home. We found one of the babies up in the rafters, bits of another behind the sink. The third they'd taken to the back of the house where they'd left what remained of him in a heap by the door. They'd eaten only soft things, like the eyes and the belly; they'd left the feet, the fused rubber fingers, the spurred, calcareous prominence of the spine. Wood rats, my father said, but later that evening Albert said no. Albert Freel read spoors like an oracle, and the droppings he'd found were small and spherical, occurring in piles like end-of-day fruit picked over and scattered by some quick, careless hand. It had to be rabbits, given the evidence. Rat droppings had a longer, less generous shape. The rat is a small-minded animal, he said. Even its feces reveal what it is.

It couldn't be rabbits, my father answered. A rabbit would never do such a thing.

All the same, Albert said, it's been a bad year. Skunk, fox, weasel – rabbit, too – everything's been living off garbage for the past four months. You know what a bad winter can do to a beast.

But they're vegetarians, my father said. They eat grass and tree bark. Forest fruits.

Look where you're living, Albert said. There's no bilberries or bramble round here anymore.

Still, when we set the traps it was wood rat we hoped for. My father had chosen the type of trap carefully, rejecting a range of more sensitive models for one which would neither injure nor maim. I imagine his intention was much as it had been the previous autumn, when he'd caught a boy stealing apples from the tree behind our house. The tree itself was unclaimed property – the land it stood on had never been ours – but the boy had crossed through my mother's garden to reach the low branches and swing himself up; the tender shoots of asparagus and aubergine, the ascending strands of the tomato vines she'd planted that spring, before she died, all had snapped with the weight of him when, awkward with apples, he'd stumbled and fallen as he made his way down. The following evening he'd come back with a basket. My father waylaid him, seized him by the collar when he tried to run away and hauled him into the house. I know you, Trevor Irvine, he'd said, then he'd made the boy sit at the kitchen table while he tried to explain about respect for others, how nothing should ever be taken for granted, how he could have had all the apples he'd wanted if only he'd called in first to ask. In the fifteen minutes before we released him I watched the blue veins at the boy's temple flutter while his eyes scanned the room for an unguarded exit, his raw reddened fingers gripping his knees.

We didn't know what to do with the doe, but my father supposed that Albert Freel would. Albert lived with his dogs and a coop of pigeons in a house at the end of the Glencairn Road. The house had been built on a crest overlooking the city, between two fields of dry gorse and heather where in the summer cows were taken to graze. His dogs were his livelihood, and he housed them with him. When my father and I came into his sitting room all six of them rose with the smooth, fluid movement of silk through a belt loop, scattering like ash to other parts of the room.

Now what did I tell you? Albert said when he saw her. What did I say all along?

So what should we do with her? my father asked him.

Whatever you want. The shops down in Smithfield might give a few quid; there's that butcher on the Road does game now and again. Or I've got a Rex out the back, if you want. Belongs to my nephew. We could try for a litter, though you never know. That might be the best thing, but, with the child and all.

Aye, let's do that, my father said slowly. Shall we do that, daughter? You've never seen wee babies being born.

Whatever youse want, Albert said. Just so long as you realise there's no guarantee.

The buck was housed with the pigeons in an ancient enclosure, one of the last thatched structures east of the Bann. Thin beams of light from the chinks in the stonework transected the space inside its four walls, casting a pattern of loose-woven baskets which moved over Albert as he stooped and shuffled, while I thought of magicians crouching in boxes, half-moons and comets decorating the sides, and wondered what they did, where they went to, when the razor-sharp swords plunged in all around.

Okay, Albert said, you can put her down here.

The buck kicked when Albert lifted it out, one hand gripping the base of its ears, the other grasping the loose skin on its back. I heard its teeth striking metal as he pushed its head down, into a cage so unfit for the both of them that small squares of pelt were pushed out through the mesh. When Albert stood up, rubbing his hands, a tuft of mahogany slowly descended, tumbling dreamily on long spider legs, and I followed its tentative passage while I listened to the rattle of metal rocking. The sound of the pigeons rose behind me, the air shrill in their talons and bright background laughter in the noise of their wings. Then an acrid smell of discharge rose from the cage, and it was over.

Albert reached in again and pulled the buck out. Give it a month, he said. If there's no litter by then you'll know nothing happened.

What do we owe you? my father said finally.

Would you listen to him, Albert said. You owe me nothing. I reckon nothing'll come of it anyway.

Somebody called for him then so he left us. I stood by my father as he gazed at the doe, feeling the weight of his hands on my shoulders and the twitch of his fingers each time his lips failed to find something to say.

You stay here, he said after many minutes, don't you move. I'm just going to go thank him properly. I'll be back straight away.

When he was gone I went to the doe. I tried to hold her the way he had shown me, cradling her hindquarters in his oversized hands, but as she was heavier than I had expected it was all I could do just to press her close, feeling the comfort of claws in her protest, the gradual relaxation in her shoulders and ears. I knelt down then, slowly, laid her out on my knees, examined the places where his teeth had bitten her, exposing the intimate undersilk to the surface like so many delicate, floss-tufted seeds. She did not flinch when I touched her, when I lifted her feet and observed their texture, the way the thick fringes of hair curled round to cushion her toes. She lay still when I held her ears to the light and traced the orchid spread of her veins, petal soft and just as intricate, the faint throb of her pulse against my hand. By the time my father returned to collect us, she had placed her paws on my chest and stood up, looking all around her with dark, intelligent eyes.

The Start of the Season

I T WAS CLOSE to five when they returned to the hotel. They'd spent the day hiking in the hills above the lake, following thin, sandy roads from which dust rose all day like steam. They'd passed the lemon trees that the brochure had described, the olive groves and vineyards, the orchards heavy with fruit and the odour of ripening. *Dear Mum,* Jean wrote as she sat on the balcony, propping the postcard against her knee. *Italy's beautiful and our room's much nicer than we'd expected. It's wonderful just to get away.*

For their first trip together outside the UK, they'd wanted to go somewhere neither one of them had been already, where everything they saw or did would be fresh and exciting and new to them both. It'd been Martin who'd suggested Italy. Jean watched him idly as he sawed at the plastic strips which bound their luggage. Israeli? the porter had asked her cheerfully as he carried their bags to their room. Tel Aviv? No, she'd told him. Belfast. They seal your luggage there, too.

She turned back to the collection of postcards in front of her. According to the guidebook they'd borrowed from the library, the post would take at least ten days to reach Britain; there was hardly any point in writing when they were only going to be there a week. The thought depressed her. *Dear Sandra,* she composed mentally as she considered another card. *So glad you're not here.* No, she couldn't write that. It wasn't her sister's fault they had to share a bedroom; she and Bill had no privacy either, after all. Jean smiled. Maybe she would write it. Knowing Sandra, she probably felt the same way.

She gathered the cards and went back inside. From the bathroom came the tap of metal on porcelain and a sudden, forceful gush of water, the sounds of Martin completing his shave. She went in and stood behind him, tracing the changing curve of shadow from his throat to his shoulder as he towelled himself dry, delighting in the smell of him, the feel of her fingers against his skin, their unaccustomed proximity to each other during rituals which they had, until then, always performed alone. In their two years together, Jean reflected, they had never shared a shower until that evening, never been able to sleep through till morning and find the other beside them, still there.

'Ready?' he asked.

'Mhm. You hungry?'

'Famished. What about you?'

She nodded absently as he tucked in his shirt, checking that the room was presentable in their absence, that all the lights were switched off and the towels in the bathroom were hung up properly to dry. Martin sighed.

'Jean, they pay a maid to do all that. You're free! You're on holiday!' He squeezed her playfully and she laughed.

'Alright,' she said, 'come on. Let's eat.'

Faint strains of music from the courtyard near the swimming pool drew them outside when they reached the lobby. There were people dancing in the garden of the hotel opposite, the couples circling slowly among heavy earthen pots of hibiscus and bougainvillea, their faces lit by the small, coloured lanterns which swung from the surrounding trees. This was the way she'd imagined the evenings, standing on a promenade above the village, watching the lights come on in the shops and restaurants which lined the marina below. That morning had been as she'd imagined it, too, the air full of fragrance and the sound of conversation from people taking coffee on the patio by the pool. It had made her ashamed of her initial disappointment, the sinking feeling she'd experienced on the coach ride from the airport the day before. For more than an hour they'd driven by houses with their shutters drawn, past deserted streets and empty marketplaces – because of the heat, the rep explained finally. Everyone's inside from noon till four. A woman in the seat in front of them had snorted indignantly, and said if she'd wanted siestas she would have gone to Spain.

The dining room was empty apart from a handful of people seated at tables beside the windows. Jean recognised some of the faces from the airport – two single ladies travelling together, a pair of middle-aged couples from the Midlands, a sizeable party of athletic-looking Germans who had arrived on a separate flight but had taken the same coach to the hotel.

'Looks like we're late,' Martin said as a waitress passed with several small plates of salad and a few egg mayonnaise. He glanced around the room, assessing their options. 'How about that table by the back wall?'

Behind them the glass doors to the lobby opened inwards, and Jean stepped aside to let the new arrival pass. 'We can't,' she said, smiling politely as the man edged past her, 'it's all prearranged. We're supposed to look for our room number.'

The man ahead of them hesitated.

'Ah,' he said, turning to Martin, 'I think you're with us. You're Room 27, aren't you? There's been two places set at our table since the first meal. I'll lead the way; we're just over there.'

It took a moment to sink in. The prospect of having company did not appeal to Jean; she'd been looking forward to enjoying the evening on their own. She looked at Martin helplessly, but he only shrugged and grinned. *Very little bothers him,* she noted as he took her hand, and wondered why the realisation left her less comforted than annoyed.

They followed the man past the Germans to a table towards the far end of the room where a woman sat alone facing the window, her hands folded across the handbag in her lap. She smiled at the man but looked startled when they, too, sat down.

'My wife,' the man explained. He and Martin shook hands

across the table, and Jean nodded politely to the other woman as they were introduced. She didn't catch their names.

'We were beginning to think we'd have the table to ourselves for the week,' the man said, looking at his wife. Jean glanced up, surprised. His tone, she was certain, had been faintly hostile, and she felt a vague antipathy surface in response.

'Yes, sorry about that,' Martin said pleasantly. 'We didn't have much appetite after the flight, and we couldn't seem to get out of bed in time this morning.' Jean looked at him crossly. *Why apologise?* she asked him silently. *We're the ones with our backs to the window. They could have left at least one seat with a view.*

'You're newlyweds, aren't you?' Martin asked, reaching for the wine. 'Somebody told me you're on honeymoon.'

'Yes, that's right. We were married last Saturday.'

'How lovely for you,' Jean said, but no one seemed to notice. She watched the comings and goings of the kitchen staff while the other three chatted about the size of the wedding, the great expense involved, the trials of farmers in Britain today, and the implications of the new Europe, but the exchange was awkward and soon lost momentum. A pair of entrées went past en route to the Germans, whose appetite was apparently insatiable and who greeted their arrival with an appreciative cheer.

'Have you been married long?' the woman asked. Again Jean felt her irritation surface. The query was, of course, entirely innocent; anyone recently married was bound to assume that all other young couples were just like themselves. Nevertheless she found the question intrusive; if the woman had wanted to avoid confrontation she needn't have phrased it quite that way. She met the other's gaze head on.

'We're not. Married, that is.'

'We're engaged,' Martin added quickly.

'Really?' The woman's expression was so genuinely delighted that involuntarily Jean slipped her hands between her knees. 'When's the wedding?'

'We haven't set a date yet,' Martin said easily. Jean's corroborative smile was tight. 'Sometime soon, we hope.' He pulled a portion from the warm loaf at his elbow, offering it to her with his eyes. She shook her head, suddenly conscious of the intimacy which could make speech between them unnecessary. *And we're not engaged,* she told him irritably, *so don't tell them we are.*

'How is the food, anyway?' Martin asked.

The woman grimaced. 'A bit rich, actually. We made the mistake of eating Italian the first night – couldn't sleep for hours afterwards.'

'We've been ordering the European option ever since, though, and that's been alright,' her husband said. 'Just be sure to ask for it well-done.'

Behind them the conversation was animated, the couples delighting in the discovery of mutual friends and acquaintances and the recollection of experience shared. At the table in front the two women had pushed aside their plates and napkins to make room for the brochures they'd collected during the day, pointing out to each other the places they'd just visited and sorting through postcards to decide which to send. Jean found herself thinking of breakfast that morning – the cheese, the fresh fruit, a few rolls from the flight, what was left of the spumante from the previous evening, the kick of her heart as they'd let the cork fly. She sighed. Still, it wasn't fair to leave Martin to cope on his own. He was being so patient, too, so charming and polite, while she kept fighting irritation and the urge to be unkind. With an effort she returned her attention to her own table.

'That's right, the Franciscan mission,' the man was saying. 'There's a museum of local history in it now. Under it, actually. In the catacombs. I can't imagine how you missed it; it was pretty well marked.'

'I'm surprised, too,' Martin answered. 'We walked around the gardens, of course, and the chapel, but we never saw a sign for a museum.'

'I have the brochure here,' the woman said, pulling a folded leaflet from her bag. Jean leaned towards him as Martin examined it, resting her palms on his forearm for balance, using the moment as an excuse to make contact. Dark, aboriginal faces stared out from the pages, their portraits appearing between shards of pottery, bone and feather jewelry, the chipped and peeling implements of tribal war – all souvenirs from the heyday of the mission. The accompanying text described in detail the primitive peoples to whom the articles had once belonged: their passion for music, their addiction to drink, their idolatrous religions, and violent, unpredictable ways.

'Thank you,' Martin said, refolding the leaflet, 'I'm sorry we missed it. I still don't know how we could have; we were right there the whole day.'

But we spent it in the gardens above the catacombs, Jean thought wistfully. At the end of a trellis they'd discovered the chapel, a small room with stone walls and a low, wooden ceiling, lit only by candles and furnished with four wooden pews. A simple crucifix hung above the altar, its Jesus roughly hewn, the two arms of the cross bound together with twine. It looks like you're praying, Martin had said, showing her the photo, a product of the Polaroid Instamatic his family had given them as a bon voyage gift. He'd captured her with hands folded, her head at an incline, gazing thoughtfully up at the cross. As he emptied the camera and inserted new film, she'd noted with amusement how he placed the discarded cartridge and scraps of silver paper on the floor at his feet rather than hazard contact with the seat of a pew. He'd been curiously self-conscious, she realised suddenly, from the moment they'd come in. *First time in a chapel, was it, Martin?* The possibility hadn't even occurred to her until them.

Behind them, the foursome were choosing pastry, deciding which of the cakes to split between whom. What's your favourite, they asked the waitress who stood beside the sweet trolley with a silver cake knife in her hand. She shrugged, her expression amiable and relaxed. Every one, *delicioso*. But there's a whole glass of rum in that one there.

The woman cleared her throat.

'So, what about you?' she said. 'Where are you from?'

Her husband's smile was strained. 'They're from Ireland, dear, obviously.'

'Northern Ireland, yes,' Jean said.

'Yes, of course.' The man lifted a sprig of parsley from the chop on his plate, examining it from a distance with the prongs of his fork. The woman coughed.

'Do you live in the country?' she asked brightly. 'I hear the country's very nice.'

'Yes, it's beautiful,' Martin agreed. 'We don't get out to see it much, though. No car, I'm afraid. We're from Belfast.' *West Belfast*, Jean added silently; she could practically see their faces blanch. For some reason she found the reaction gratifying.

'Ah yes,' the man said, swallowing deliberately. 'Right in the thick of it, then.'

'Well, it does seem that way sometimes, I suppose,' Martin laughed, 'but it's not as bad as all that, really.'

'Are there really armed policemen and tanks on the streets?' The woman's expression was avid, and uneasy blend of fascination and distaste. And what about the bombs, and all those shootings, the woman continued; do you think it would stop if they brought back hanging? Jean leaned aside as the waiter moved in to serve their first course, keeping her eyes on the man's white sleeve and deft fingers, trying to listen only to the light tap of silver against glass as the warm strands of pasta were scooped from one dish to the next. Such discussions always brought out the worst in her. Inevitably she made some radical and accusatory comment with whose sentiments she did not really agree. But what're they fighting *about?* she heard the man say then, and Martin spoke calmly of politics and history, of cultural differences and conflicting aspirations, of each side demanding protection without understanding that the other was equally afraid.

'And what side are you on?'

Jean looked up. She'd been waiting for that question; in fact, she was surprised that they'd waited this long to ask. Martin struggled to find words for a diplomatic answer; she knew she was being childish but she would not return his glance.

'We can't help being curious, I suppose,' the man said. 'We don't meet too many of you, really, not in Dorset. Aren't you on our side, then?'

Jean set down her fork. 'And what side is that, exactly?'

'We like to think we're not on any side,' Martin said quickly. Jean felt him grip her knee under the table, and she crossed her legs tightly to push his hand off. The other two nodded but said nothing, apparently waiting for him to go on. Martin shrugged and smiled. 'We try not to be, anyway.'

The man looked puzzled. 'But surely you're from one side or the other.'

'Well, when you put it that way,' Martin said, 'I guess we're from both sides. We're a mixed couple – Jean's a Catholic, I'm Protestant.'

Oh, for chrissake, Jean thought bitterly, *must we tell these people everything?* She felt an irrational urge to say something inflammatory, to embellish the reality of her own experience and imply activities in which she had not been involved. But then Martin would stop in the middle of his answer – how they were pacifists who had met through the peace movement, how nobody they knew had ever been injured, how nobody close to them ever had died.

Shamed by self-recognition, she hesitated. The other two were nodding their heads while Martin described how careful they'd been in the early days of their courtship, the precautions they'd taken and yet still been on edge – preoccupations which after two years no longer mattered, replaced by others far less exotic, which even Martin, with his broad-minded notions of privacy, had the sensitivity not to bring up. For a moment Jean saw herself as she imagined they saw her: pale-faced and silent, clutching her napkin, overcome by a topic too painful to discuss.

She avoided their gaze as the plates were cleared, as they finished their coffee and brushed crumbs from their laps, as they gathered their room key and other belongings and finally rose to leave. When they had gone Martin covered her hand with his and sighed.

'Well, that wasn't too bad,' he said. His voice sounded weary but she did not respond. 'D'you fancy dessert?' he asked, changing the subject. 'Ice cream or something?'

'We're going to get one anyway; it comes with the meal.'

He eyed her warily.

'What is it, Jean? What's wrong?'

Though she'd given him all the usual signals – the cheerless expression, the imputative silence, the refusal to meet his eye – the speed with which he'd responded to them took her by surprise. For a moment she wavered, considered aborting the mood, but she still felt the tug of unrealised conflict and a gradual tightening between her brows.

'I just wish you hadn't said that,' Jean said, despite herself. The tone of her own voice only irritated her further. Martin's expression was grim.

'Said what, Jean?'

She gestured impatiently. 'All that stuff.'

He shrugged dismissively, withdrawing his hand. 'We've been through this before, Jean. What difference does it make what we say to them? Come Saturday morning we'll never see them again.'

But that was in Belfast, she countered silently, too unclear in her own mind to argue out loud. *You expect to field questions from strangers at home.*

'I think,' she said stiffly, 'you had an obligation to be truthful.'

'And how wasn't I, eh? What did I say that wasn't true?'

She shook her head, suddenly inarticulate. 'And why did you

have to tell them so much about us? I don't know them; I don't want them knowing my business.'

He nodded. 'So now I was too truthful, is that it? Tell me something, what would you have said? Eh?' She didn't answer. 'No? Well, I can guess. My way, they go home thinking at least some of us aren't terrorists. Your way...? I don't understand your way at all.'

Most of the other guests had already departed; only one elderly gentleman was still sipping coffee at a table by the door. A girl from reception was moving among the tables on the far side of the room, clearing cups and emptying ashtrays, her white blouse sheer and loose and unbuttoned above the bosom, bright orange beads around her neck swinging out from inside it as she cleaned. Jean watched Martin signal for coffee, admiring the clench of his thighs as he turned – his *sartorius,* she told herself tenderly, his *rectus femoris.* He was right, of course; she was overreacting. She should learn to take these encounters less seriously, to be like the ones who gave tours of the building sites, pointed to the corrugated iron erected to keep the kids out of the unfinished bungalows with which the Executive was rebuilding Ardoyne and said, See how the Brits make us live? Bloody tin shacks with no running water. It's worse then South Africa here, so it is.

Jean smiled, remembering how she'd first heard that story, how she'd told it to Martin and how he'd laughed, too. Bright and unburdened, she turned to him then, but he was examining the sugar packets in the bowl on the table and would not look up, and just as swiftly as they had come to her, her good spirits drained away. Outside the evening pressed like paint against the window, and all she could see as she looked into the glass was her own reflection, the image clear and remarkably well-defined.

Hydrophobic

E DDIE CRANSTON ASKED my sister to marry him three times
before she stopped saying no. The first time he'd come
with flowers and gone down in front of her on one knee,
even though he was a big man and the position was difficult for
him. The second time he asked her he put it in writing and then
stood on the corner across from our house, so she'd know where
to find him when she wanted to look. A postal strike delayed the
letter but still he kept standing there three days in the rain – which
impressed her enough that she went out to him, told him directly
that he was a heathen and there must be no mingling of the
heathen and the saved. So he said that he'd do whatever she
wanted, anything at all if it made her change her mind. That's
when she told him about the Holy Spirit, the need for forgiveness
and a cleansing of sin. That should do it, my father had said, turning away from the window and shaking his head. If he's got any
sense now he'll give up and go home. But instead Eddie told her
he'd think about it, and in the end said Okay, if that's what it takes.

We were eleven days now from the end of February, and I was
thinking that the water would be cold. The grass beneath us was
brittle with frost, and the ice spread like filigree from the banks
around the water, reaching out like fairy fingers towards the belly
of the Lough.

How you doin? Eddie asked me. You okay?

I nodded. How you doin? I said.

I'm okay, he said. I'm alright.

I didn't believe him. For a man who couldn't swim he was
taking it very well, but I had felt the cool damp of his skin when

he took my hand on the way into the church. I knew he was afraid.

It was too early, really, for an outdoor baptism. The only one I'd ever seen had been in the summer, two dozen people in white robes with Bibles standing face front to the Irish Sea, lapped by the water and equidistant like the driftwood pillars of an obsolete pier. We'd spent that day in the Sperrin Mountains, were on our way back along the Antrim coast, headed for Whiteabbey where the hospital was when my sister saw them and made us pull over for a better look. There was a family of swans in the reeds by the water, an elegant female and three grey cygnets; my father and I stood watching them till my sister called us over, crouched down beside me and made me look along her arm. Reminds me of Emily, my father said – my Aunt Emily who had been to Israel, who had gone with her church to the Dead Sea. When the bus had stopped to change a flat tyre practically everyone had stripped to their swimsuits and offered their wounds to the heavy brine before reboarding the bus and going on to En Gedi. Only my aunt had remained on the shore, where she stood with their cameras and other possessions and watched as the rest of the congregation descended until they were nothing but knobs of saffron, ash-grey, and auburn against the even, eggshell green of the Sea. She'd gone in later when they got to the Spa. You can't drown in it, she told me, the water won't let you. One minute you're standing, just touching bottom, and the next something starts to upend you, lifts you up by the balls of your feet and tips you over; you keep coming up whatever you do. And you can only stay in for a little while, or the pull of the minerals saps all your strength. Once you come out you go straight to the showers, and then you can sleep, or buy ice cream, or a lovely tall glass of something cold to drink. There had been some, she said, who'd refused to shower, who, having bathed in the salt tears of Jesus, would not give them back to the Sea. Fools, my aunt had called them, fools to let their faith eat away at their skin.

Two readings had been chosen for the opening service,

Deuteronomy 7, the first five verses, and Luke 12: 49–53. We stood and sat down several times in the course of it, then the service was over and the hymn had begun.

Well, Eddie said, I guess that's my cue.

He rose and leaned forward to edge around past us, obstructed by an uneven battlement of knees. My father turned to look after him as he headed up the aisle, but I closed my eyes and imagined his movements, thinking, *He's in the foyer now with the rest of them; there, they've just handed him a robe.* I imagined him undressing behind a curtain in the vestry, the lift first of one leg and then the other, each sock rolled individually and tucked, one each, into separate shoes. I wondered if he took off his shirts like my father, both hands reaching round to tug at the garment and pull from behind with a crackle of static, or if he crossed his arms in front of him the way I did and took hold of the hem, his face distorted by the snag of the buttons or reddened for a moment by the chafing wool. Then the organ pipes swelled and the full force of them reached me, a thousand throaty voices answering every pressed key, the space in which to hear them filling with sound from one end to the other like water fills an ice cube tray.

When the hymn finished we all moved outside. A wind was gathering on the edge of the water; it moved confidently among the assembled, tousling hair and examining gowns, lifting hems and cuffs for inspection before moving on. My sister stood to one side and consulted her Bible; even the wind seemed to know better and give her a wide berth. Here, daughter, my father said softly, go see how he's doing. So I went over to Eddie and took hold of his hand.

How do I look? he said.

Cold, I said. Do you know what you're supposed to do, now?

You tell me again, he said.

There is one body and one Spirit, I said, one Lord, one faith, one baptism, one God and Father of us all, who is above all and through all and in all. That's all you need to know, I told him. Please don't be afraid.

There were three to be baptised, two women and Eddie, and as they were church members he'd agreed to go last. The first woman sank back in the water like a slumberer, surrounded by the cushions of air in her clothes. I remembered how my sister had washed a coat once without having emptied its pockets first. Eighty-five quid and a bill of sale, all that was left of some forgotten transaction my mother had made before she died came out in a lump, and we had to submerge it in a bowl of warm water till the layers separated and the creases relaxed. That's what it looked like, that jellyfish way the cloth sank and lifted just below the surface. Then there was another time when they'd let us out early, told us not to ask questions and to head straight for home. The police had been there, and the army, too, but still Jimmy Macken had torn leaves from his textbook and hurled them in celebration straight back at the school. A gust of wind had lifted the pages, pressed them up into the bare limbs and branches of the trees in the schoolyard. The next morning they hung there dripping with rain, and that's what the woman's arms looked like, buoyed up beside her in the cold clasp of her sleeves.

When she resurfaced, the water ran off her in all directions with the soft spit and sigh of a bubble breaking. The deacon caught hold of her wrists as she straightened and gave her a push as her eyes scanned the shore, a little shove to get her started as she struck out towards whomever she'd come with, waving, bright pearls of water sliding off of her skin.

Ah, your poor sister, my father said. We both knew my sister had wanted this for herself. Standing once in the corridor just outside the ward, I'd heard her describing her plans to my mother, the changes she'd make in the way she'd been living, the difference that Christ had already made in her approach to things, good or bad. I'd listened to their voices, rising and falling like gulls in strong wind, until my father returned with three cups of coffee and a glass of orange from the hospital canteen. Whatever brings you strength, my mother had said, whatever you trust enough to believe. But then her church had acquired a transparent tank with internal wiring, waterproof lights, and a set of steps with a handrail leading down, and though she'd considered moving to some other parish, eventually she'd reconciled herself to a second birth indoors. Poor thing, my father said, it's been hard for her, too.

The next woman, taller, lay back in the Lough like a plank of wood. When she righted, the water broke over her arms first, then her face, burbling from her mouth and nostrils, twist-spinning off her hair; she was smiling. The minister helped stand her erect, kept his hand at her elbow as she moved away, until the swing of her arms as she walked through the water pulled his touch free and other arms reached out towards her with towels, welcoming her back to the shore.

Then it was Eddie. I heard the tide hiss and swallow on the sand as he entered, and made up my mind not to take my eyes off him until I was sure he was going to be okay. I'd asked him once why he'd never learned to swim, and he'd answered quite simply, I don't like the water. I know in the absence of riptides and whirlpools the odds of drowning are very slight, but still I'm afraid of being pulled under, of stepping suddenly out of my depth. You must think that's awfully silly, he'd said. Not at all, my father'd said. There's no one I know who isn't afraid.

When I was younger, I'd spent a week on a peace camp with Catholics, one of several cross-community ventures to be held that summer in Ballyclare. The leaders who had organised it had stood each one of us on a four-foot stump the second day, had us fold our arms across our chests, close our eyes and fall backwards stiffly, into the arms of the rest of us below. I remember the sensation of gathering momentum, the surge of my heart and the heaviness behind – and then the clutch of many fingers, my clothes tightening like sheets snapped taut, and the hard heels of hands, buoying me up. A trust fall, they'd called it. There'd been twenty-eight altogether, fourteen of them and the same number of us, and we were almost through it when one of the boys had refused to participate. No one would do anything after that, and the rest of the week went trying to remember just how much each one of us had told the others, wondering what they'd do with the information, wondering if we'd given too much away.

My own ears filled as his went below water. The sound of everything suddenly grew thick, as when I lay in the bath with my head submerged listening to the subterraneous whine of a tap in the kitchen, the soft, hollow whisper of my knee on enamel, or the low, cetaceous echo that answered when I knocked on the floor of the tub with my heel. I held my breath when I saw him go under, felt fire spread from my heart to my lungs to the pit of my stomach, my whole body brimming with a flammable gas, my joints swelled, I could see only udders, old tubes of toothpaste, bakers in white hats filling pastry with cream, and I gasped. When I opened my eyes Eddie's arms were reaching up through the face of the water, and I thought of a picture I'd seen of some famous fountain – Laocoon and his sons encoiled by serpents: their fingers, too, had been sharply angular, just so had the water around them heaved and churned. From the top tier the gods had looked down through the windows of heaven, and wide jets of water had streamed out from their mouths.

Later, back in school, we'd tried it ourselves, the trust falling. There'd been no stump so we'd stood in a circle and taken turns being in the middle and allowing ourselves to fall back against the crowd. But part of the circle was weaker than the rest; it did not surprise me when at last I broke through. It seemed to take ages before I hit asphalt, and as I was falling I imagined them watching, caught off-guard by their error, observing the breeze in the force of my fall.

He came up choking. Even as he left it the water dragged him down. He'd thrashed so much all three were sodden – Eddie, the minister, and the deacon as well. When they reached the shore with Eddie between them, my father was there, and together they lay him out on his back a few yards from the water. Then my sister got down on her knees in the sand beside him, and when she had loosened the clasp at his collar she took his chin in one hand, his nose in the other, covered his mouth with her own and kissed him, kissed him, till his eyes fluttered open and again he breathed.

Departures

M Y FATHER DID the double the year that Harry died. By the same reasoning that led him to drive his brother's car only on Saturdays because he had no licence and was not insured, he worked only part-time to minimise his chances of getting caught. As a strategy for survival it worked remarkably well, and he could have gone on that way forever, had Harry's nephew not turned him in.

My father was fifteen years in the city before he moved into the house beside Harry's. The second son of a man whose farm was neither large nor rich, he'd had no choice but to leave the country and try his luck away from the land. At twenty-three he'd taken a bus from Ballymoney to Belfast and arrived in the city just as the shops were closing. He'd walked from the depot to the centre of town amid the sluggish flow of people emptying out of offices and into the streets. In search of a boarding house or a YMCA he'd hired a taxi and headed west, to the home of a girl the driver knew, a girl from the Shankill who lived alone and took in lodgers.

When I was old enough to appreciate romance, my father would speak to me of her as any aging artist would speak of what was once his inspiration. Her name was Madelaine Andrews, and she had just turned twenty when they met. She was tall, slim, and glamorous, with the wide, liquid eyes and the full, pouting lips so favoured by the fashion-conscious of a later era. Her hair was long and auburn, and so unreasonable that she wore it where it fell, or else piled it up haphazardly. In every way she defied expectation:

she was bookish, yet beautiful; privileged, yet unpretentious; street-wise, but unbruised.

The only child of a defiantly mixed marriage, she, like her parents, had made a name for herself as an independent thinker, unfettered by the fads and mores of the moment. At a time when those of her peers who had not embraced some form of Christianity had rejected their gods altogether, she would not join the rush to declare what she believed and why. At eighteen she had moved out of her parents' house and found a place of her own with two other girls from school. Six months later they left to get married but she stayed on alone, readying the rooms and airing the linen and opening the house to any lodger, male or female, who happened to apply.

My father's previous experience with the opposite sex had been limited to brief, ungainly contact with certain farmers' daughters at the infrequent functions his local parish held; he had never met anything like her before. As a child I loved the story of their meeting because it was in its telling that my father's powers as a speaker were most pronounced; yet at that meeting Madelaine struck him dumb. She spoke incessantly, but in a low, mellifluous voice so pleasing that he could not describe her talk as chatter. On the stairwell she explained that she did not own the property, the government did, and that strictly speaking she shouldn't be hiring out the rooms. My father had been raised never to touch things not his own, and such things included the law. Yet with one month's rent already paid and the keys there in his hand, the uncomfortable feeling settled upon him that he'd already committed a crime.

In the small, white bedroom at the top of the house he'd unpacked his belongings while she set his books out on the mantle. Having inspected their titles she asked to borrow Kavanagh, and as she was leaving with the book under her arm she'd cast a final glance over his collection and remarked that she, too, was an ornithologist. He'd looked at her blankly. You like birds, don't you? she'd demanded. Uncertainly he'd agreed. Well, then, she'd said, as if all had been made clear, you're an ornithologist.

The next morning she broke the rules of her own establishment and made him breakfast. She also pressed his trousers, polished his shoes, and lent him a tie. My father was a handsome man when he was young, well-mannered and polite and clean about his person; but he had never dressed for an interview before, had no idea what to wear or how to behave, and the unfamiliar made him awkward. Madelaine, who enjoyed the process, adopted his cause as her own, fussing over his appearance and advising him what to say, and arranging to meet him in the town that evening to hear how he'd gotten on.

Perhaps it was his country accent, or perhaps he simply wasn't qualified for the jobs for which he applied, but in the weeks that followed my father could find no work at all. Occasionally he was short-listed; now and again he had an interview, but eventually he grew tired of filing forms to no avail and resigned himself to being unemployed. For a while he spent his time in the hills above the city with his books and a flask of tea, but eventually the weather disowned him and he was forced indoors.

Madelaine was an indifferent housekeeper. She liked to keep the floors swept and the porcelain surfaces in the bathroom clean, but dusting bored her so she never did it. She was a competent but unenthusiastic cook, preferring simply to stock the kitchen and have her guests prepare their meals themselves. Gradually, and without intention, my father took on the minor chores: he'd collect the soiled linen, recreate the unmade beds, or push a broom around the kitchen whenever he grew restless or whatever he was reading temporarily lost appeal. He'd been doing this for more than a month when Madelaine approached him one evening after tea to suggest he abandon his search for a job in the city and look after the house full-time.

It was easy work, and after weeks of frustration and disappointment he accepted with relief. He did the shopping, the cooking, and the washing up; he boiled the tea in the morning, kept track of the lodgers throughout the day, and in the evenings secured the door and banked the fire before he went upstairs to bed. In return for his services, Madelaine allowed him room and board, and finagled him free membership at the private library where she worked. Within the year she'd agreed to be his bride.

My father's marriage did not alter his circumstances or improve his attitude towards his surroundings. The arrangement did, however, provide him with the companionship of a partner who understood and sympathised with him. My mother knew that had it been possible, her husband would have returned at once to his father's pastures; indeed, he never would have left them. Her own wish was simply to leave the Shankill for anywhere else at all, though why she was so desperate to leave was never very clear. By way of explanation she would say only that she didn't like the people, and since she had grown up with them, antipathy was her right. It was true she had never found her niche among the women of the Road, that the schoolmates and relations with whom she'd been most friendly had long since moved to Dublin or crossed over to Stranraer. It was true, too, that she valued her privacy and disliked the tradition of unexpected visits which was so much a part of life on the Road. And yet so many people knew and liked her that the greeting cards we got at Christmas could cover the surface of every sill and end table, while others hung from lengths of ribbon which each year spilled down like bunting over the branches of our tree.

Every Wednesday on her day off from work she would go down to the Housing Executive to enquire into the status of her application for a transfer. She knew every official and representative by name, and would pester them with phone calls and letters until they either transferred or retired, or departed this world for the next. To whomever replaced them she would send a note of welcome and a copy of her file, but still she wasn't moved.

My father would accompany her on her weekly visits to the

Housing Executive, and before Stephen and Nicola were born and I was left at home to mind them, my support was enlisted as well. During these interviews my mother refused to be put off by the kind of excuses that invariably silenced her neighbours. If the files had been lost or the computer had gone down, she had her own copies with her in her bag. If the application forms had been updated and she had to resubmit, if there were no places available in the locations she preferred, even if they told her outright that there was nothing wrong with her present situation and she lacked sufficient points to move, still she would not back down.

Standing just out of earshot with my hand in his, my father and I would watch her through the glass which separated one consulting cubicle from the next and strain to hear as she made the odd suggestion as to how to improve the quality of the service they provided. Do this, she appeared to be saying, gesturing at the collection of cranky children and chain-smoking adults that filled the waiting area behind her with no clear idea of the order of their arrival or who was next in the queue, and all *that* will disappear.

As the years went by without progress on her case, the younger staff would joke with her and tell her that when they built the next branch office, they'd let her cut the ribbon and crack open the champagne. Get me that transfer, she'd tell them, and I'll let you name it after me.

My parents had never planned the size or contours of their family. Occasionally, while they were courting, my father would imagine himself in the company of the children they would have, but he hadn't thought about when they'd have them or how many there would be. My mother, so savvy about other matters, was like a child herself about this. After I was born, they greeted the confirmation of her two subsequent pregnancies with a mixture of bafflement and joy, each having thought the other had taken precautions. Whatever contraceptive she eventually employed following Nicola's birth, it proved effective for nearly six years, until she discovered she was going to have a baby at the age of

34

thirty-nine. She was dumbstruck, having naively assumed that childbirth wasn't possible for a woman nearing forty. And, for her, it wasn't: she took pains in her seventh month, alone in the house on a Saturday in June. Eight days later she was dead.

My father blamed himself, even before it was over. Theirs had been a reversal of traditional roles in every respect but one, and it was in this sense that he felt he'd failed her. The day before the funeral, when the transfer from the Housing Executive at last came through, my father seized upon it as her dying wish.

Ever the optimist, my mother had long ago packed most of her belongings into sturdy cardboard boxes, the contents of which she had inscribed in capital letters on the outsides, all in anticipation of an imminent move. Though impeccably itemised and arranged, each box was a haphazard collection of items, apparently grouped according to owner rather than function. While another woman would have put the kitchen items in one box, the contents of her wardrobe in another, her business papers in a third, my mother had piled sketch pads, chequebooks, perfume, lingerie, hair lacquer, a coffee mug, and a dozen other things together in the same box and listed them all under the heading, MINE. My father dug out that box, and the two others like it, the night her body was prepared. For the three days that followed he sat on the floor of the bedroom they had shared, the contents laid out neatly in rows in front of him, softly turning the pages of her books, running his fingers along the dark, heavily punctuated scribbles she had pencilled in the margins, and refusing all offers of food. Then he packed them all up again and sealed them with tape, and when he was done he went down to the Housing Executive and took the first thing they offered him, sight-unseen, so anxious was he to escape from the house that reminded him so much of her.

They gave us a flat, one of sixteen identical units in a large, four-story block which itself was one of many constituting the Glencairn estate. Each block was a warren of tunnels, overpasses, stairwells, and hallways with silent concrete chambers jutting out on either side. Every corner on the ground floor of every block stank of stale beer and urine; above, the smell was of old potato peelings and laundry dried in small, airless rooms.

A stairwell led from the makeshift car park at the side of the building to the third-level corridor onto which all the upper flats opened, and ours was one of these. It had two bedrooms on its second floor, a kitchen, a sitting room, a bathroom, and a toilet beneath the stairs. It also had what can only be described as a decorative balcony, presumably our compensation for the small back garden we'd been promised but never received. If it had been positioned in front of either of the bedroom windows rather than astride the empty space between, we could have stood on the balcony and viewed the whole city, and perhaps even beyond: the soft curve of Helen's Bay, the dull orange lights of Bangor, the majestic double outline of the Harland and Wolf cranes, the ship-yard, Central Station, and even, on clear evenings, the momentary flash from the lighthouse in Donaghadee. But in fact the balcony was no more than a sheet of corrugated iron, bent in at the corners, painted a sad, coagulated red, and welded onto a floor-less iron frame which protruded some distance from the wall.

All the same, to me, as to my siblings, Glencairn was an estate like any other. It had a chippy, a winemart, and a healthy propor-tion of children under fourteen. But to my father, who could still recall a time when phone boxes and petrol stations existed unmo-lested on the Road, when one could travel freely between the Shankill and the Falls, and when, every spring, there were swans in the Woodvale Park, Glencairn epitomised all that was wrong with the city. It was large and dirty and prone to garish displays of colour; its stench assailed his nostrils and made his stomach turn; outside its windows the rumble and grind of passing buses kept him sleepless and on edge. That he had made the move himself only tortured him further, for he knew that she, too, would have been unhappy there.

In Glencairn the privacy she'd so valiantly defended was impossible to maintain. The estate was composed of a few extended families, each member of which kept the others informed as to the progress of their pregnancies, the state of their marriages, and their prospects for employment, immigration, and death. Even for an outsider it was almost impossible to take any action without the whole estate knowing of it in advance. A young unmarried couple occupied the flat next door, and during the day we could hear every syllable of their conversations as clearly and effortlessly as they could hear ours. They'd been allotted the flat because she was three months pregnant, yet despite her condition, they made love nearly every afternoon as soon as he returned from work. The day my father came upon the three of us kneeling together on the unmade bed, clustered round a plastic beaker which we had pressed like a stethoscope against the wall, he resolved to go back to the Housing Executive and request again that he be moved.

Things might have been easier had my uncle not refused to visit us, fearful of the vandals and joyriders who were known to do damage to cars in Glencairn. When the farm dried up after my grandparents died, my uncle had sold the land for all he could get and about twice what it was worth to a pair of amateur genealogists, and then moved, not to Belfast but to Bangor, where he'd invested in commercial property, a corner pub with a fish-and-chip shop attached. When my mother was alive my uncle would leave his entrepreneurial interests occasionally and drive down to Belfast in his Volvo. With a benevolent air he'd hand the keys to his younger brother and, walking briskly for the benefit of his health, would head off into town on foot. When he was gone we'd load up the car, and my father would drive us out to the place where he'd been born.

The farm's new owners still lived in America and used the property as a holiday home only once or twice a year; my mother was sure they wouldn't object to our parking the car and laying our picnics in the fields behind the barn. We would chase rabbits and my mother would read, holding the book at arm's length above her to block out the sun, while my father wandered off on his own. Occasionally, when he was a long time returning, my mother would set off to retrieve him, and once, after they both had been gone for over an hour and the colours and sounds of evening were well under way, I left Stephen and Nicola in the backseat of the car and headed out after them myself. They were pulling dry burrs and grass seed from each other's clothing, and I nearly missed them, because the grass had grown tall by the stream where they lay and their voices were so soft at first I could hear only water. But I told you that story already, he was saying. I know, she'd answered. So tell me again.

As he could offer no more convincing a reason than my mother had for his sudden request for a transfer, the people at the Housing Executive were civil, but unsympathetic, and they soon wearied of his forlorn presence in their waiting rooms. It was because they refused to rehouse him that my father decided to squat. On Saturdays and Sundays after our dinner we would wander the broken streets of the lower Shankill until my father found a site which struck his fancy. There were many to choose from, for all the old estates in the area were scheduled for demolition, and most of the inhabitants had already been farmed out to new and improved dwellings further up the Road. One forgotten house looked very much like another from the outside, but inside the remnants of identity still littered their floors and clung to their plaster. In some the carpet remained, soaked through with rain from above and damp from below; in all, the shadows of past furnishings could be seen in vivid silhouette against the faded wallpaper that had surrounded them. As we went around the rooms we would point these lonely patches of colour out to one another, vying to see how many each of us could name. A mirror, a picture, perhaps a wall clock – the simple geometry of circles and squares could have indicated any one. The larger outlines of wardrobes, headboards, and bookcases were easier to distinguish, as were the few whole walls still brightly patterned, protected behind units in which the china, silver, and trophies of a lifetime had once been displayed.

The site upon which my father finally settled was the first house in Park View Terrace, just off the Woodvale Road; it had belonged to a policeman before they burned him out. Unlike the houses of the lower Shankill, it had not been stripped of wood for the bonfires in July. Its doors and window frames were still intact; the rafters did not stretch like naked ribs between the roof space and the open air. No animals, furred or feathered, had settled in before us. Though for nearly a year it had lain empty, only a few splashes of graffiti adorned the iron sheet the authorities had used to block the door. While the parlour was uninhabitable because of the smell of petrol and charred upholstery, the fire had not gone beyond that room, and the rest of the house was practically new.

Squatting was a concept that would have appealed to my mother. She had always enjoyed defying authority, and though she would never have imposed her rights over those of others, she was prone to take a creative interpretation of what those rights entailed. Her convictions ranged from the fantastic – she believed it was everyone's right to drive, with or without a licence – to the enigmatic – she abused expense accounts on the grounds that, had she not been working, she would not have been making the purchases she did – to the ideological. Once, in the midst of some school project and flummoxed by flow charts and graphs, I came to her to ask about taxes. She shrugged apologetically and told me she never paid them. My father looked up with the air of a man who had just discovered that something he had believed to be settled was still a matter for debate.

'No, and I will not, either,' she said defiantly, more to him than to me. 'Why should I pay for what I don't want? I didn't vote for them; let them pay that did.'

My father, who had struggled unguided through Locke, Rousseau, and Hobbes, dropped his head into his hands.

'We're all citizens of the same state, Maddy,' he said, 'and if that state provides – '

'No,' she said. 'When I get what I vote for that's when I'll pay.'

My father was convinced that she would have liked the house in Park View Terrace. Long ago Woodvale had been a posh place to live, and some vestiges of that respectability had yet to disappear. Most of the residents were pensioners with small private incomes who kept fairly much to themselves. Even next-door neighbours who had known each other since childhood confined their contact to a polite nod in passing or a brief, amicable exchange of words. Almost everyone was a self-professed Christian, and though my father all his life preferred to worship God not in His house but in His fields, he had respect for commmitted churchgoers. Be kind to the Christian, he once told me, and God may be kind to you.

'But it doesn't matter if you're not a Christian,' I'd told him smartly. 'If you're not a Christian, you just won't be saved.'

It was the night of All Saints, and on the other side of the room my mother knelt with pins in her mouth preparing my sister and brother for the evening's masquerade. Her fine brows were knit with annoyance, directed not at the children but at the stubborn fabric which defied her fingers and seemed bent on wasting her time. My father watched her for a moment, silently deploring her impatience but observing her determination with an admiring eye; then he turned back to me.

'Don't you believe it,' he answered. 'God knows who they are that love Him best.'

The short row of buildings of which the house he chose was one sat at the junction of Bray, Broom, and Enfield Streets. None of these was used frequently despite the proximity of a popular Chinese take-away, which every evening from four o'clock on caused the aroma of chips and fried onions to hang heavily on the air. It appeared that my father's quest for domestic isolation had at last come to an end, for there was only one other house in the strip which was not empty, and the occupant of that house was Harry.

Although he was not a helpless man, Harry was effectively deaf. He was also crippled with arthritis and had been pronounced legally blind. After eighty-three years of remembering to do a great many things, his memory had at last begun to fail. On occasion he forgot to take his pills or to carry his spectacles, or insert his hearing aid and his teeth. My father, who had vetted the area fully before deciding to move in, produced his assessment that Harry would be a quiet, unobtrusive neighbour. He listened to his wartime records with the earphones plugged in as he couldn't hear them any other way, and he did the same with the radio and the TV. He spent most of his time brewing tea the way his wife had taught him, with loose leaves and water just boiled, and when it was made he sat in his front room in an armchair by the window with a plate of biscuits and read the paper. In all the time my father had his hopeful eye on the Terrace, Harry had received only one visitor, a small, fat man with quick, impatient gestures and a high-pitched voice. This, my father had discovered, was Harry's nephew, George.

Geordie Bellam was known locally and by his own definition as a small businessman; the diminutive suited him well. He owned a fifty-pence shop at the bottom of the Shankill which made no profit, and all of his money was tied up in its stock. He was in competition with three other bargain gift and toiletry shops, all of which had sprung up like weeds after he had established his, and all of which were owned and operated by Pakistani immigrants. He lived alone somewhere in Lisburn, though most evenings he slept on the floor in the unfurnished flat above his shop, so convinced was he that 'the Pakis' were plotting to destroy him. For protection he had installed an expensive sprinkler system and an electronic, high-sensitivity alarm, but he refused to take the cheapest and most reliable option and simply get a guard dog. Having grown accustomed to being responsible for nothing but himself and his merchandise, the thought of having to feed or care for anything else annoyed him. It was only natural that he would resent being burdened with Harry when the old man's wife passed on.

Harry's wife Eleanor had been a clever woman, and she'd known her nephew well, but even she had not been able to plug every loophole in her will. She had stipulated that if Geordie valued his inheritance he would have to 'provide' for Harry, but she had not required that he provide for him himself. When we took over the abandoned house beside Harry's three months after Eleanor died, Geordie was still trying to rid himself of his uncle. He had by this time discovered that all Harry's cronies were dead and that most of his neighbours were in the same state of decrepitude as Harry himself. The list of people requesting home help or the attention of a social worker was a long one, and Geordie was not inclined to wait. The only option remaining was to have his uncle taken into care, but as there was nothing seriously wrong with him he could not be institutionalised without his consent, and this Harry simply would not give.

Harry was proud of the fact that he had no need to move. His wife had seen to it that the house in Park View Terrace was indisputably his and that everything in it was in his name. Moreover, Harry did not want to move. He and his wife had been married in that house; his daughter had been born in it. He had christened his grandson in the Presbyterian church around the corner and had walked with his son-in-law in the park across the way the night before he'd immigrated to Australia with Melanie and the boy. Harry watched the changes in the photos his daughter sent and which he carried with him whenever he went out. The boy had grown bigger, every year taller and with ever more chestnut hair. Melanie was fuller, more like a woman than the girl he had reared, but still she sent her greetings to the neighbourhood as she did to the friends from her childhood she had left behind: Who looked after her garden now that Mrs Baird had died? What about the Stadium – had they finally torn it down? And Olive Street, Yew Street, Ottawa and Chief – were they all still there and the same as before?

His daughter wrote to him faithfully every fortnight, and Harry would read her letters aloud to his nephew as soon as they arrived. The wee girl's counting on me, George, he'd say when he finished. How could I move away?

Geordie soon tired of his cousin's abject affection for the Road. He visited his uncle as infrequently as possible and begrudged him even that small fraction of his time. Yet despite his appearance Harry was quite fit for his age. His bones were not brittle, he had never smoked, and with luck, the doctor had told his despondent nephew, he could very well outlive them both.

Geordie had a reputation for seizing opportunities, and he did so with ferocity. Our arrival in Woodvale was just such an opportunity, for my father was the candidate for whom Geordie had been searching: neither too old nor too young, in perfect health, conveniently located and seldom away from the house. Moreover, he was economical. Squatting was illegal; far from demanding a wage in return for his services, my father could be induced to provide them for free, in return for Geordie's silence.

Though my father never spoke of the arrangement, Geordie made sure that it was well-advertised. The butcher, the grocer, the doctor, the chemist, the girl at the bank – all were provided with the new information that my father, not Geordie, would be acting as Harry's emissary from then on. Overnight he became a public figure, beseiged by a notoriety for which by nature he was utterly unprepared. In the past he'd been known largely as Maddy Andrews's husband, and he had been happy enough in his own identity to accept the other without distress. As he had grown older people had noticed him less and less; after my mother died he went out so seldom he might not have been there at all.

Accustomed, then, to anonymity, he now was forced to exchange greetings, or worse, make conversation, with every convoy of pram-pushing women and battalion of men who had ever known Harry, Geordie, or any of their relations. Errands which used to take him at most two hours to accomplish now took him at least four, and often much longer still.

Rather than simply play along with Geordie, agree to every imposition without comment or complaint and then, once he'd gone, just continue as before, my father became obsessive. The old man was just as he'd predicted, quiet and undemanding, yet no matter how much my father did for him, he felt his efforts were inadequate, that somehow he deserved to do more. The irony was that looking after Harry need not have involved a great alteration in my father's way of life. When my mother was alive no workday passed without his having something waiting for her when she got home – a new book, or flowers, or a moderate bottle of wine – and with us he was just as generous. If he went shopping in town he always returned with sweets for Nicola and socks or pants or running shoes for Stephen, whose energy soon outdistanced every pair he received. For me he would bring things in installments too expensive to purchase in one go; I remember a microscope, a doll's house, and the complete works of poets and playwrights he'd recommended that I read. He would willingly have done the same for Harry even if Geordie had never found us out. As it was, he did no more for him than he had done for his wife and continued to do for us now that she was gone; he simply took no joy in what he did.

My father blamed no one but himself for his ability to be blackmailed. He accepted his predicament as a punishment just and sound, though gradually he recognised his need for at least a temporary reprieve. He couldn't, however, reconcile himself to abandoning Harry without legitimate cause; a job, he decided, would be a good excuse to get away. Moreover, he needed the money: he'd bought food on credit and an anorak for Harry, and he owed money to the local electrician who had hot-wired the house for us before we moved in. All those bills still had to be paid. When he heard that the Wimpy's near the City Hall was hiring, he enquired in person and was amazed when he was offered a job.

The franchise preferred its product to be sold by attractive young women, so only they got jobs behind the registers. Those less fortunate were assigned to folding boxes lined with grease-proof paper in the back recesses of the kitchen. The more intelligent of the young male applicant pool were placed on the fryolators and grills, while those with acne, unusual hairstyles, or unseemly tattoos were hired to wrap the burgers and arrange them on the warming shelves behind the counter. My father, a bit of an embarrassment in his undersized overall and red-and-white striped cap, was relegated to sweeping the floor.

He was given the night shift on Mondays and Wednesdays, the two slowest evenings of the week, and his wages were paid in cash. It was his request that we stay away from the Wimpy's on the evenings he was working, although once, against his wishes, I did go to see him there. I knew what it was that made him find it so demeaning, and I had wanted to tell him that he had no reason to be ashamed. My mother had always objected to uniforms of any kind, and had discouraged us from professions in which all employees were required to look the same. While clothes, she warned me, could not make the man, they could sometimes tell him what kind of man he was.

And yet my father did not mind his job, I think; so I left before he saw me, and without speaking to him as I'd planned. Protected by the invisibility too often accorded those engaged in menial tasks, he had no need to speak to anyone, and no one spoke to him. The noise of scolding parents and of orders placed and altered did not disturb him. The restaurant had two levels, both of which were partitioned into smaller areas by the artful arrange-ment of large, white troughs of plastic vegetation. From four o'clock until midnight my father moved his mop from one end of the place to the other, taking a ten-minute break every so often to wait for the floor to grow littered with cartons and cold chips before he started the process over again. At the end of eight hours he changed his clothes and went home, through the silent town with its derelict arcades and grim police patrols, up the empty, unlit Road to the house.

In so small a city as Belfast, it was inevitable that Geordie would discover that my father had a job, and when he did he could barely contain his glee. As far as he knew, the government offered no reward for turning in squatters, but informing on those who were working while claiming to be unemployed paid fifty pounds per head. The first night he came to our house to gloat, he lingered on the doorstep for a full twenty minutes while our dinners cooled and the dust from the street blew into the hall, leaning against the doorjamb and smoking through his teeth and chatting about times getting tough, making ends meet, doing whatever necessary in order to get by. Every so often afterwards he'd drop by unannounced to comment on the few additions my father's wages bought and which Geordie's keen, intrusive eye invariably managed to spot. When he was gone my father would sit as if physically drained. In the end, unnerved and anxious, he turned to his brother for advice.

My uncle's response was typical. In the days before experience had honed his business sense, he had accepted a brown and yellow, five-berth caravan as partial payment for property he'd bought, then sold; this he now proffered for our use.

His voice cheery, unwilling to accept the problem as real, he suggested we get away for a while, have a holiday, forget about the whole thing. He'd run us down himself if we wanted, and we could give him a ring when we wanted to leave.

Caught up in the spontaneity of the notion my father agreed, though he made sure to look in on Harry before we left. The caravan was just outside of Newcastle, usually a popular seaside resort. But in early March it was still dark and sparsely populated; few people cared to spend their wages in a town with little else to offer than a few enshrouded amusement halls and a fitful, troubled sea. Even at peak season my mother had always preferred Portrush. She liked to walk the path beside the bed-and-breakfasts where the wind was strongest and the smell of salt water was sharpest on the air. There was a set of swings at the far end of the most distant pier, and it was there we could always find them, once we'd eaten our fill of candy and ice cream, had gambled our pennies on the miniature horses, and had no more money left to spend. I stayed with them once when I was too sick in the stomach for food or for rides and watched them play. With hair unpinned she shook her head at him – Don't go so *high!* – and he stood behind her, just out of her reach, sometimes pushing gently, sometimes catching hold of the swing as it came back to him and clasping her tight around the waist so that she sat suspended for a moment with her feet unable to touch the ground before he let her go and she swung out again towards the sea. Don't *push* so high, she'd tell him, and then she'd pump her legs madly and make herself go higher still.

There were swings at Newcastle, too, but only the frame remained, the seats and chains having long ago disappeared in that mysterious way to which most public facilities seem prone. While my father waited at the bottom of the slide with outstretched arms, I held Nicola's hand as she slid down to meet him and told Stephen when he asked me that the swings were inside for the winter and if we came again in spring he could play on them then. It was warm for the season and we stayed late, loathe to ring my uncle and get ready to leave. When we got into Belfast on Sunday night it was after ten, though the light in Harry's parlour was still on. My father could see him seated at his desk and decided to leave him be. By half past the hour we were all in bed.

When my father found him the next morning Harry was

already three days dead, blue-skinned and as stiff and straight as the chair he'd died in. His expression in death was neither peaceful nor disturbed; he'd had a heart attack while replying to his daughter, yet neither of their letters revealed anything that would have brought it on. While Stephen fetched the doctor, who rang the hospital and the police, my father gathered the pages and put them away with Harry's other papers before the officials arrived. When they got there, the constables took my father's statement and the doctor took his pulse, checked us all for signs of shock, and sent someone down to find George. Then the medics took Harry away.

I remember the funeral and the viewing before it as a pathetic affair, dimly lit and poorly attended. Geordie had not bothered to ring his cousin in Australia, having decided, under the circumstances, that the funeral should take place as soon as possible and with the minimum of fuss. Harry had no family left in Belfast to make recriminations or to raise the issue of Eleanor's will, but Geordie knew the accusations were sure to come as soon as Melanie heard the news, and he had no intention of being taken unprepared. Even before he'd seen the undertaker he'd paid a visit to his solicitor to discover if his share of Harry's savings had been compromised by the death.

In a room with mustard walls, plush russet carpeting, ornamental brass fixtures, and casual, sling-back chairs, Harry's coffin was incidental, its lid propped up behind it against the wall. The four of us arrived in the same black frocks and trousers we had worn when my mother died and had not put on since. Following my father's example, we each peered briefly into the coffin and moved our lips like his before going on to clasp the cold hands of Harry's nephew, who sat alone in the front row and accepted our offers of sympathy without a word. In the hallway where we waited while they nailed the coffin shut, I watched my father turn to Geordie and begin to speak, but Geordie cut him short and turned away. The solicitor stepped in then, a tall man in an iridescent suit. Something made me leave Stephen with Nicola and cross over, imbued with a sense of purpose I'd seen once on my mother's face when she'd defended my father against a man who'd pushed him outside a restaurant in Shaftsbury Square. We'd gone out for supper on a wet night when I was still the only child, and after the meal we called a taxi to take us home. The man came out from a bar across the street and stood for a moment swaying in the rain before he came over to us. Orange bastard, the man said gratuitously, and then he'd pushed my father and knocked his glasses and his hat to the ground. My mother raised her umbrella with both fists around the handle and swung it down from behind her head as a blacksmith smites an anvil, and the man fell down in front of her on his knees. During the ride home she sat between us, holding a handkerchief to my father's bleeding temple, one arm around his shoulders, the other around mine. The tears were bright against her cheeks yet I could see no trace of anger in her eyes. I stood in the doorway of their room as she put my father to bed; then we went downstairs and she made us both a cup of tea.

'That's not the way, you know,' she said. Her hands at last were trembling, and she did not look at me as she spoke. 'Your father'll be sure to tell you so tomorrow, so I might as well say it first.'

Geordie's solicitor was just leaving as I touched my father's sleeve. 'My advice to you, mister,' he said in parting, 'is to stay out of the way. You've dealt my client here a serious blow, a very serious blow indeed. Let's hope for your sake it's not more serious than it seems.'

'What's he talking about?' I demanded, and even called after him, 'What've we done?' but neither of them answered. Within a week the authorities had found us and had begun proceedings against my father for the money they said he'd stolen while claiming to be unemployed.

At the burial my father stood apart from the small assembly – the grave digger, the minister, a few from the Road still able to walk, and Geordie – and we stood by his side. Just as he had said, 'This is it,' five months before when at last he'd introduced us to our home, so he now turned round to us as they lowered Harry's coffin and said simply, 'This is death.' I think he believed that, for all my mother's funeral had been a grand affair. There had been music and laughter at the reception, platters of food and a great deal of drink, a final triumph of one tradition over another. Everybody who had ever known her came, and the rooms were filled with the aura of reunion, not of loss. I could feel my mother's presence there as clearly as I had when I was a child and she had held me and spoken to me as she gently stroked my hair. I imagined I could see her, leaning against a bookcase, a glass of wine in her hand, looking on with satisfaction and distaste as we sang and drank in front of her. I tried to tell my father that, for the sight of him, bent and lonely in a chair by the door, surrounded by colour, by texture and sound, made me throb with sorrow and the wish to give comfort. But I was young and inarticulate; when I told him I could see her he grasped me by the arms as I stood before him and shook me, asking where, where.

Stigmata

THE COMPLEX CONSISTED of twin towers, each fifteen stories tall, each equipped with a single payphone in the lobby and a set of four washer/dryers in the basement beside the lift shaft. There were eight units on every floor, each designed for a single tenant with little time to spare; the rooms were small, and with only two to choose from, time spent in the flat could pass slowly. Each unit on the ground floor had its own tiny, self-contained garden, the false appearance of the semi-detached.

It was the garden that had attracted Eileen to the flat in the first place, that and the convenience of the complex to a depot from which she could catch the bus into town. She'd seen its potential when she first viewed the property, had pictured the look of the blossoms and hedges as she gazed out the window, her mind moving on to the cost of the necessary implements even as she agreed to the terms of the lease. Yet in the end she'd found little time for gardening. She'd dug the hard ground with the shovel she'd purchased and spread it with grass seed as the packet instructed one Saturday just after she'd moved in, but though she'd been there a year and a half already, still nothing had taken root.

It was the third evening she'd worked late that week, and close to eleven when she turned from the footpath towards the first block of flats, digging for her keys. Though she was proud of her reputation as a reliable worker and considered the last-minute requests of employers less imposition than a sign of respect, she'd been finding it difficult lately to maintain the pace. Fatigue made her stupid; she dropped things in public, ordered coffee when she meant to say tea, in the evenings discovered stains on her person which must have caused comment during the day… And she mislaid things. She was still rooting around in search of her keys as she scraped the bolt back across the low, wooden gate at the foot of the garden and turned around to face her front door. It was only then that she saw the man.

He was slumped across her doorstep just inside the alcove, his arms tightly crossed against his chest, his chin buried in the folds of a thin, grey scarf, his face half-hidden by the hood of his anorak. When she saw him she started violently and cried out, more from surprise than from fear. But then panic did grip her and she stumbled frantically back to the gate, struggled again with the rusty bolt, and scrambled round to the other side, slamming and bolting it behind her, deafened momentarily by the sound of her own breathing.

Despite the disturbance, the figure in the doorway had not stirred. Gradually his inaction bolstered her courage; if he'd meant to attack her, she decided, he would have done so by now. After all, she'd been standing practically on top of him just a moment before – even now she wasn't much more than a few feet away – and he looked to be a big man, one who could easily have grabbed her before she'd had the chance to scream.

From the far side of the fence she called out to him.

'Hey,' she said softly, straining to distinguish his features in the uneven, amber light. She called again, louder this time, but still he did not move.

Cautiously, and with as little noise as possible, she slid the bolt across and stepped slowly around the gate, closing it softly behind her. Even so slight a reduction in the distance between them brought him more sharply into focus. From the little she could make out he might have been an attractive man once, even imposing. A small knot of tension throbbed suddenly at the back of her neck. She took a step closer and leaned towards him.

'Hey, are you alright?' The figure rolled slightly at the sound, like a moored ship against a wave. Eileen stepped back quickly, but the movement hadn't wakened him. A sudden thought struck her – Perhaps he's dead. Inexplicably the thought made her giggle. There would be an inquest, of course, and then the funeral, which she would pay for and which only she would attend. She thought of the fistful of earth in her hand, the touch of the veil against her cheek, of the questions that'd be asked of her when she returned to the office, a black ribbon round her arm, of the office girls clucking and fussing and making her endless cups of tea…

She shook the images away, suddenly annoyed. She strode the two steps over to where he lay, knelt down, and gingerly prodded his arm with her bag.

'Hey. Hey, listen. You can't stay here.'

The figure did not respond. Eileen released an exasperated sigh, uncertain how to proceed. She was clearly conscious only of the cold, of a loss of sensation in her toes and fingers, but she was nevertheless impressed by the absence of the expected. Puzzled, she put her bag down beside her and gently laid her hand on his sleeve. She was inches from his face, and the soft sound of his breathing now mingled with her own, yet there was no smell of alcohol, no stench of perspiration or of filth accumulated over time. She could see now that he was roughly her own age, somewhere between thirty and forty. His hair was an unremarkable brown, of varying length and irreversibly thin, the scalp of an invalid in rapid decline. Despite his bulk, his limbs appeared fragile, too slender to sustain their own weight. And yet his cheeks were not sunken, his face not as gaunt as she'd first imagined. She'd seen faces like it in hospital beds; both her parents had worn it briefly towards the end. It was an in-between face, potentially, from under which familiar features could resurface or be replaced altogether. She saw herself suddenly, laden with fruit juice and flowers, the night nurses whispering at the far end of the ward, the matron's gentle touch on her shoulder pressing her back into her seat by his bed, the sound of the curtain drawn close around them, the doctor responding without hesitation, I understand; of course you can stay.

The path and overhanging vegetation to her left was lit momentarily by a haze of white light, and Eileen heard the sound of tyres twisting up the driveway to the block. At the same time she sensed a sluggish movement in her direction; the man was leaning like a tree about to fall. She stared at him for a moment, watching his gathering momentum and wondering how it could possibly fail to disturb his sleep. When his shoulder touched hers she panicked; she dropped her briefcase beside her bag and pushed against him with all her strength, but he was the heavier and hers the more awkward position. She lost her grip and slumped onto the path, legs splayed, skirt hitched up above her knees, supporting his head uncomfortably in the crook of her arm. From the car park came the sounds of footsteps on the gravel, a car door slamming, the exchange of cheery farewells. Light swung away in an arc from the path as the car reversed, turned, and drove back the way it had come, and Eileen heard laughter and the sharp, military click of stiletto heels as whoever had been the passengers now headed towards the back of the block.

They were a young couple in their mid-twenties, stylishly dressed for a night on the town. He had his arm around her waist and was pulling her close, his mouth against her throat, his free hand wandering. Then the girl saw Eileen and pushed his hand away.

'Here, Arthur,' she said indignantly. Her companion murmured something and clutched at her blouse. She slapped his hand down. 'I thought you said this place was posh,' she accused, nudging him and straining away from his embrace. The boy glanced up briefly and took advantage of her lingering footsteps to run his hand along her thigh.

'Please,' Eileen said, struggling to disengage herself, but her throat was dry from disuse. The man in her arms moaned softly, shuddered, and turned his face towards Eileen's coat.

'C'mon, Arthur,' the girl said abruptly, her voice rising. 'C'mon, let's go.'

She pulled away from him and hurried on down the path. Her sudden urgency pleased the boy and he ran after her, hopping on one foot for a moment as he readjusted his trousers and ran his fingers through his hair. Eileen heard them laughing as he fumbled with the key. Then their door slammed shut; the light from their sitting room stained the footpath till they drew the curtains and the whole block grew dark and silent once again.

With difficulty Eileen checked her watch. She thought of the door at the back of the block, and behind it the central staircase from which all the flats in the block could be reached via their emergency exits. Without a special key the door could be opened only from the inside; as a consequence it was used mainly by repairmen and tenants in the upstairs flats who had motorcycles or other heavy gear which they preferred to store inside. In the eighteen months she'd been living there she'd never had occasion to use that back entrance; the caretaker had pointed it out to her when she first moved in. He'd not been a particularly friendly man, civil during working hours, yes, but hardly accommodating on weekends or after five. What his reaction to her present predicament might have been at a quarter to midnight on a Thursday she didn't like to think. In any event it was irrelevant; he'd left the job three weeks before, and no replacement had yet been found. There was no one else to whom she could turn.

It was her own fault, really, she thought darkly. She should have gotten to know her neighbours. As it was she didn't know anyone else in the block; in fact, apart from the caretaker now departed, she didn't know anyone in the estate at all. She'd tried to be friendly if she ran into others while doing laundry, but, like herself, they'd kept to themselves. She'd assumed they were busy, that their days were ordered much as hers were, with little opportunity to invite others in. Besides, she'd never expected to need their assistance; if there were repairs to be made or a problem to be sorted out, it was the Council to whom the matter was properly referred.

Given the late hour it was unlikely that the stairwell would be in use; still, it was worth a try. Proceeding with caution Eileen eased the man back against the wall then rose stiffly to her feet. He still slept, but fitfully. The hood of his jacket had fallen away from his face, and she stood for a moment, watching his lips and eyelids tremble like liquid carried from one place to another and thinking, It should be such an easy thing, to simply reach past him, unlock the door, climb over him, and go in. If he fell into the entry when it opened, he could stay there till morning. The flat's inner door had been fitted with a pair of locks by a previous occupant; she'd be in no danger with those firmly in place.

'It should be easy,' she said aloud, and then sighed, and headed for the back door.

She hadn't expected it to be open; security on the estate was quite good, and such an oversight would have been unusual. But she had expected some response to her knocking; surely the sound of a shoe on an iron door would have alerted someone, somewhere? But fifteen minutes passed and a light, drizzling rain began to fall and still no one appeared. Damp and hoarse, with stockings torn, she was on her way back down the path towards the front of the block when the door opened. A young man in unbuttoned jeans and a worn dressing gown held it ajar with his foot and hurled a bag of rubbish some fifteen feet over the wall of the low, roofless enclosure opposite, into an unseen bin. Eileen heard the clatter as the bag made contact, knocking a lid onto the concrete floor behind the wall. The boy gave a quiet, self-appreciative cheer and turned to go back inside.

'Hey, wait a minute!' she called after him, squinting against the bright fluorescence of the hallway light. 'Hold that door a minute, will you?'

She stumbled up to the step, conscious of her disheveled appearance, but the boy did not seem to notice.

'Forget your key?' he asked cheerfully, shivering for effect as he pulled the door shut behind them. The query was rhetorical; she opened her mouth to answer but he'd already turned away. He was halfway up the stairs when she thought to call him back.

'Excuse me, I don't mean to pry, but have you been in all evening?'

The boy stopped and looked down at her. He nodded shortly.

'It's just that there's a man at the side there,' Eileen explained, 'I thought you might have noticed him – '

Instantly the boy became solicitous.

'Why didn't you say so? Where is the bastard?'

'No, no, it's nothing like that. He's just a man lying there on the ground.'

'What, in the foyer?'

'No, outside on the step. My step, actually. He's been there for twenty minutes at least. I just wondered if anyone was doing anything about it.'

The boy looked puzzled. 'What, like ring the peelers?'

'Well, no, not exactly. I don't really know what one ought to do under the circumstances. Frankly I was thinking of going in through the back way and leaving it at that.' She grinned sheepishly, hoping he'd sympathise with that approach. 'Perhaps the police are the best bet, though. I really don't know.'

Her indecision had not impressed him. She could sense his interest in her story flagging and the return of his desire for whatever awaited him in his own flat upstairs. 'It's alright,' she said, suddenly weary, 'it doesn't matter. I'm sorry to have troubled you.'

Again the boy nodded, his eyes scanning her face and figure as if he were only just then taking them in. 'Alright then?' he asked dismissively, resuming his climb.

'Yes, thanks,' Eileen answered, though she knew he wasn't

listening. 'I'll just get in through the back.'

'There's a phone out the front,' the boy said aggressively on the first floor landing, 'but it only takes five p's.'

'Thank you,' Eileen said again. The boy went inside and the door swung shut behind him. Eileen leaned heavily against the banister and dug her keys out again, then went down the darkened corridor, lit only by the luminous glow of the exit sign and the coloured lights of the electricity panel beside the lift, till she reached her own flat.

Once inside, she pulled all the curtains and double-locked the inside door. When the place was secure she stood for a moment in the dark, listening. Then, moving swiftly, she switched on the lights, the radio, and the TV, and both electric fires. Then she showered, changed, and filled the kettle. It was only then that she allowed herself to think about the man.

She couldn't just leave him there, she saw that now. Still, it would be foolish to bring him into the flat, however harmless he might have seemed. It didn't seem fair to ring the police; they weren't likely to treat him gently, and after all he hadn't really done anything to warrant a complaint. She stood up with a sudden clarity of vision and found the cardboard box with everything she'd salvaged from her parents' house before the place was sold. There at the bottom were the old blankets and pillows they had used on camping trips when she was a child. She brought the items into the kitchen and made two mugs of strong, milky tea, extra sweet, covering his with a saucer to keep it warm. She'd place the cup beside his head, she decided, where the scent and the steam would be sure to wake him, and she'd put the blankets over him and leave a pillow by his arm rather than disturb him while he slept. Perhaps she could even sleep in the sitting room, on the settee, to be nearer to him in case he needed anything in the night.

The front door was heavy and swung inwards; she'd need both hands to get it open. Leaving the light in the entry off so as not to disturb him, she set the cup, the pillow, and the blankets on the shelf above the mains and slowly, very carefully, eased the door open so he wouldn't tumble in. It took her more than a minute to open the door that way; by then he was gone. The garden was empty, the step was bare, and though she scanned the car park and called out for him repeatedly, he was nowhere to be seen.

Touched

THIS IS WILLIAM EMMONS ringing, he said. He thought the animal might be dangerous and could my father come right away. It was late so I'd answered, recording the details in the notebook we'd bought in Belfast the day before. You see? my father said when I woke him. I told you it was worth holding on to that phone. It wasn't until we were halfway there that he remembered, and then he nearly stopped the car and turned around. But we have no rabies here, he told me. There are no rabies in Ireland.

The Emmonses were an elderly couple who lived on their own outside of town; they weren't the type, my father reasoned, to be involved in pranks. We'd had a number of hoaxes in preceding months, usually clear as such from the start but not always. They'd sent a child once, a six year old with curls and dimples, who'd told my father that her mam was suffering from delusions, that she'd even tried to cut her own throat. She's in the kitchen now, mister, the child had said, and she's got my daddy's gun. When we got there the woman was preparing supper, bent over a pot with a ladle in her hand. A crowd of boys had gathered to watch us, but they were afraid of my father and what he might do to them, and they'd run off as soon as we left the house.

The old man and his wife were waiting by the road for us when we arrived. He stood up and came over as my father stopped the car.

You alright? he asked, and the old man nodded. Well let's get to it, then. Which way?

Emmons's wife stood behind him, grey and illusive against the darker, oleaginous black of the night. Her husband turned to her and they spoke briefly; then together they stepped into the crossed beams of our headlights, becoming for a moment a pair of pale trousers in unlaced work boots, a dark skirt in bedroom slippers, nothing more. They lifted the latch from the cattle guard and stepped forward, pushing the gate in front of them like a plough. We left the car where the gravel drive ended and followed the soft crunch of their footsteps along a dirt path which led to the barn.

It was an ancient, ruinous structure, about two hundred yards from the house. The animal, Emmons said, whatever it was, had been in there for hours. Around midnight he'd heard noises, the sound of glass breaking, what could have been buckets and tools overturned, and he'd gone to investigate. Something had hissed at him and seemed to lunge forward; he'd heard fangs coming at him so he'd bolted the door and run back to the house. An hour or so later when he'd listened for movement he'd heard snarling and foaming and agony instead. It was his wife who'd remembered my father's name, who'd found the number and had him phone us.

Beneath us the path was lit up like a runway by potholes and wheel ruts filled with rainwater, each one reflecting a trembling white stain of the moon. Emmons stopped outside the barn.

Just open it? he asked.

Yes, I think so, my father said. But let me go first.

The air was cooler inside, and damp. Fine grains of dust twisted like slow falling stars in the shaft of light from the single window, settling amid shapes of stacked crates and equipment which blunted the far edges of the room. Crumbling bird nests clung to the rafters and the floor was cobbled with guano and down. My father glanced around quickly.

Is there a light switch?

The man and his wife looked at each other in confusion. No, the man said, I'm sorry, no.

Anything will do, my father said quietly. A torch if you have one, even a candle.

Again the old man looked at his wife. After a moment she nodded, turned, and headed back towards the house.

Should I stay, Mr Leary? Emmons asked. But my father was walking forward again, his eyes fixed on a point beneath the stairs that led up to the loft. Even from the doorway I'd seen it too, the brief, incandescent, lighthouse flashes shining green, then amber. Gradually, as my own eyes adjusted, I distinguished the outline of a long, slender muzzle, large ears upright and inquisitive, the sound of swift breathing, the occasional glimmer of something wet. My father put his palms on his knees and bent down.

There; there now, he said softly. It's alright.

We waited that way for Emmons's wife. Soon I could hear the slap of her shoes on the pathway, then the light from the storm lamp she carried seeped under the door like milk around my feet. My father stood up slowly.

That's fine, he said. If you'll just leave it right there.

Anything else, Mr Leary? Emmons said. Is there anything else you need?

Just look after the child, my father said. See she doesn't catch cold.

Poor motherless orphan, the old woman said, you poor wee thing. So tightly did her skin cover her that every knob and protrusion of her skull was visible, hard-edged and jagged, revealing her teeth in a rigorous grin. Her hair was so white as to be transparent in the glow of the lamp her husband held behind her, her face sunk in shadow, her eye sockets cavernous. The bulbous joints of her fingers were level with my face as she clutched at her shawl, and I thought of tight sacks of marbles and the four iron feet supporting our porcelain bath at home.

It's going to be alright now, my father was saying. Don't be afraid.

Can you see what it is, Mr Leary?

It looks like a fox, yes, my father answered. A frightened wee fox, not rabid at all.

The old man shook his head. Imagine that, he said. Just a wee fox causing all this trouble.

My father was speaking more softly now, shifting his balance from his thighs to his fingers, gradually adding the stalk of his forearm, then his shoulder's bulk, allowing the strain to collapse his knuckles, rolling forward on the slow, heavy wheel of his weight. At the same time the animal's breathing had become less laborious, and the shrill, anxious wheezing I'd heard when we first entered had all but disappeared.

Emmons set the lamp down on a barrel and leaned in for a better look. The old woman's claw was on my shoulder, I could feel her press me forward, could almost taste the yellow smell of her in the air. My father stretched his hand towards the fox with the palm opened outward, and I watched its rich, russet pelt glow warmly copper, rust mixed with cinnamon, threaded with bronze.

God Almighty, Emmons said. He too had seen the thin crust of dried spittle on the fox's dark lips, the brown, matted mark of drool on its chest.

The old woman grunted. Your father saved that girl, she said, he made that young man see. I was there. I saw him do it.

I'd been there, too. At least eighty people had been in attendance, and the aisles had been so crowded with wheelchairs that had there been a fire we all would have burned. He'd hired a hall in Randalstown, or rather, someone else had hired it for him, had charged ten pounds for general admission and presented my father with fifty in cash. This was after he'd seen Our Lady crying, her blood-bright tears travelling lazily over scratched plaster cheeks. She'd raised her eyes from the fallen Jesus and looked right at him; two days later he'd seen her hand move. Other mourners had been on their knees beside him; they'd been the ones to tell the priest. Only the local papers had been interested until someone remembered his talent for healing, how he set broken limbs, could lance an abscess, how he'd eased my mother's pain a little, before she died.

There now, my father said. He'd been holding his hand in front of the fox, offering his odour to its quivering snout. Now he slowly withdrew it, rotating his wrist as he did so, presenting the broad back of his hand with its five outstretched fingers, waiting to pass muster before carrying on.

Alright now, alright, he said. There's nothing to be frightened of. We're almost finished, we're almost there.

I tried to see your father in Ballymena, the old woman said, but we couldn't get in. Then all that trouble after... She shook her head. Don't you listen to them, wee girl. They're a jealous lot. One religion or another, it makes no difference to the Lord. Your father made that child well again, he drove those evil spirits out. That's the way I heard it, anyway. No one can blame him for the Devil being strong.

The child had been epileptic. His father produced him in the middle of a seizure, bore him straight to the stage as he kicked and shook and laid him down, saying, Drive this demon out. The crowd went quiet while my father cried and pressed his fists to his temples, saying, Ah Jesus help me. But he'd placed his hands on the child's brow, put his fingers inside the red wet mouth and held the slippery tongue down, saying, Hush, hush now, holding the boy so tightly that the trembling had ceased and the boy had grown calm, the wild drumming of his heels on the floor had stopped, the frantic fish-flapping of his hands had died away, and his father had clasped my father's hand, saying, Thank you, Jesus, for my only son. Then the meeting went on for another three hours while they brought my father their cancers to touch, their sores and their rashes and their open wounds; and for a moment even he believed he could cure them by placing his hands on their swollen fingers and twisted spines. But then the boy had had another seizure and they'd driven my father from the hall, crying, Charlatan! Swindler! Bastard! Taig! Boys outside had broken our car windows and we barely managed to get away.

Buried in fox fur, the foreshortened fingers robbed his hand of its usual grace. My father's caress was barely perceptible, stirring only the long, stiff bristles on the animal's shoulder, not even touching the skin. Behind me the old woman was muttering softly, and I heard the abrupt resumption of her husband's breath.

The fox's lips parted. I watched them rise, furling back heavily like curtains lifting from a stage. Then the wall of white teeth split open, I could see the dark tongue beginning to writhe, the animal's head was rushing forward, its eyes had locked onto my father's and its teeth were sinking into his arm.

And then the old woman was screaming and her husband was lunging for a pitchfork or a hoe while the light from the storm lamp careened over the walls of the barn and sank into the hay. I could see my father grasping his bicep like a tourniquet, his arm bent at the elbow and the fox resisting his pull, its forelegs stiff out in front of it, its haunches dug in, its eyes never leaving my father's, even now, worrying the wound slowly, deliberately, like a man who smiles as he shakes his head, No.

Outtake

T HE BUS LEFT him off near the post office in the centre of town. From there he walked through to Cornmarket, then down Ann Street to the club. He'd been there before but never on his own, and not for some months. The last time he'd come he'd been with Gibbons and Fitz; there'd been no chance of getting a girl with the two of them around. The best bloody pickup joint in Belfast, Jimmy, Gibbons had called it – then gone and picked up everything there was to find. Wherever they went it was always the same: what Gib didn't want Fitzy would get, leaving Jim on his own for most of the night. The last time they'd been out together Gibbons and Fitz had walked out with a redhead each. Jim'd bought a few drinks for a ginger-haired girl who he'd thought had seemed interested, but in the end he'd gone home alone.

He knew what his problem was, of course; he wasn't a smooth talker. Gibbons had a clever tongue, and Fitzy played off him. Together they made a formidable team; there was simply no room for Jim when the other two went into action. He'd considered going out on his own once or twice, but somehow the idea of breaking up their partnership had always seemed disloyal. The three of them had grown up together, gone to school together, been in fights together against a whole range of rivals, foreign and homegrown; it didn't seem right to fall out over something as foolish as who had more luck with the girls. But then Gibbons had been done for armed robbery and Fitz's girl got pregnant, and the responsibility for the decision was taken out of Jim's hands. Nobody could expect him to wait around for the child to be born or for Gib to get out on parole, especially not now that he was working again and had a bit of money for a change.

He paid the two pounds to the bouncer and jostled his way through the crowd to the bar. With a pint in each hand he weaved between tables and around couples locked in embrace until he found a free corner to set the glasses on. The air above the dance floor was thick with perspiration; condensation had formed on the lights which hung from the ceiling, and the shadows of the droplets speckled the bright splashes of colour on the floor. He drank deeply, surveying the room over the rim of the glass and bobbing self-consciously to the band behind him. As always the music was painfully loud; in the brief pause between numbers his ears rang with a thin, high-pitched sound, the same whine that lingers from a sharp blow to the head. Above him the strobe lights spun off a blond girl in sequins who stomped and gyrated below. Not bad, he thought. She'd've turned Gibbons's head. *Hold me back, Jimbo; temptation's in motion, and I'm giving in…*

'Would you believe it's all for the drummer? You'd not see her up there if the D.J. came back.'

There was a girl beside him, small, dark and trim, watching the blonde with sisterly concern.

'You know her?'

'Oh, aye. We're together. We're mates from school.'

She continued to stand beside him, calm, relaxed, the sleeve of her blouse just brushing his arm. He cleared his throat.

'So she fancies the drummer, then?'

'Not half. She's only been to every gig he's done, and he's in three different bands at the minute. It's cost me a flippin fortune, so it has. And I'm not that keen on them myself.'

She shook her head, smiling, her eyes still on her friend. Jim stared at her mutely, wondering if he'd met her somewhere before. It seemed so easy, talking with her, not at all like the conversations he usually had with girls. Perhaps she'd mistaken him for someone else? Puzzled, he glanced away, caught sight of his open mouth in a mirror and quickly clamped it shut.

She was drinking wine but her glass was nearly full so he couldn't offer her a drink. He wanted to say something but his mind was cluttered with the too familiar. *Come here often? Cigarette?* The music stopped in a tangle of wire and steel; the band announced a ten-minute break, and the dancers reluctantly dispersed.

'Here she comes,' the girl said. 'Don't let on we were watching her, now.'

The blonde was headed in their direction, fanning her flushed cheeks with both hands. She seemed to know a great many people, and her progress was impeded by the young men and women who reached out or hailed her as she passed. Someone was showing her a wallet-sized snapshot when she caught her friend's eye and made a face, plucking at her blouse.

'Jeezuz, it's effin hot in here!' she said as soon as she reached them. She exhaled loudly, her breath cider-sweet. She looked parched, and his own glass was nearly empty so he swallowed the rest hurriedly and turned back to the women with a nervous smile.

'Do youse want somethin?'

The blonde pushed the damp strands of hair away from her brow with a languid gesture and looked him over, her eyes strolling. Then she craned her neck around him as if he blocked her view and scanned the room beyond.

'Here, Angie,' she said, 'was Gerry lookin for me?'

'Now, Denise, I haven't a clue. I've been speaking to this fella here. I didn't bother with the band.'

The blonde shrugged and smiled dismissively, then turned back to Jim. 'Alright, then,' she said, 'mine's a Pernod and lime. What do you want, Angie?'

The other girl shook her head. 'I'm alright, thanks.'

'You sure?'

'Go on, Angeline. Have somethin expensive.'

'We'll be over there,' Angie told Jim firmly. 'And you, don't be cheeky.'

When he came back with the drinks the two women were seated at a long crowded table against the far wall. Denise was chatting with great animation to the boy beside her, and even Angie was smiling and nodding in the company of someone else. He felt a pang of disappointment, unexpectedly strong. But the women parted to make room when they saw him, and though the glasses sloshed dangerously he managed not to spill any as he squeezed his way in.

'The band?' he asked Angie. He handed her a fresh glass of wine and she smiled.

'You didn't have to, you know; cheers. Anyway, I don't know who theseuns are. They were here when we sat down.'

Denise twisted round to him, her hands still on the other boy's knee. 'Ta,' she said, raising the glass he'd brought her. 'Ta very much. What do they call you, anyway?'

'Jim.'

'Right, Jim. We're doing a survey. Which do you prefer – bikini briefs or boxer shorts?'

'What, for fellas?'

'Would you go with a woman who wore boxer shorts, Jim?' She elbowed the boy beside her and he grinned.

Jim thought for a minute. 'Boxer shorts, I suppose.'

'And why's that, Jim?' Denise asked seriously. All the boys at the table were grinning now, too. 'Choose one: A, comfort. B, style. C, easy access.'

Jim smiled stiffly while the others laughed, his embarrassment turning rapidly to annoyance. I should've just kept away from this one, he thought bitterly. Now the other one'll think I'm a fool.

'Take no notice of her,' Angie said, 'she's always a bit mad on a night out. She's alright really, when you get to know her.' She smiled. 'So. Tell me about yourself. What do you do all day?'

So he told her about the new job, about his boss and the other lads, about what it was like to drive a fork-lift compared to a car. She was still learning, she told him, didn't like it much, found changing gears the worst. Cars were too expensive all around, they agreed, but it was worth it to be able to just get up and go away. They chatted about holidays and where they'd travel if they could, about the price of airfares and houses and how they liked to spend their money when they had any spare to spend. She was a waitress, she said, in a Chinese restaurant in Botanic Avenue, and the tips were desperate.

'What, you work with all them Chinks?'

She pursed her lips. 'With the Chinese, yes. It is a Chinese restaurant, after all.'

The concept was genuinely interesting. Jim set down his beer. 'But isn't it ... you know. I mean, aren't you the only ...?'

Angie laughed, then sighed and looked at him as if she were trying to think of a simple way to explain something which should have been perfectly clear. 'You mean the only white girl?' He nodded. 'Well, actually, Denise works there, too.'

Jim snorted; he could just see that one serving up prawn crackers and chicken fried rice. He shook his head. 'I couldn't do it.'

Angie shrugged. 'They're just people, Jim, same as you or me. Anyway, you get used to it after awhile.'

The band returned, and the throb and pulse of music shook the room again. Jim moved closer to Angie, positioning himself so he could listen as she spoke and watch Denise at the same time. Her handbag sprawled on the seat between them, revealing a compact and lipstick, a few crumpled tissues, the wide plastic teeth of a purple comb, and a photo of herself looking much younger without any make-up, sitting cross-legged in front of an armchair, a laughing infant holding onto her sleeve. By accident she jostled him and they both apologised, Jim out of shame, fearing he'd been caught on. But Denise had linked arms with the boy beside her, and Jim watched as she dipped her glass down the front of her blouse and rolled it slowly against her skin. With difficulty he looked away.

'Here, you,' Angie said. 'She'll be alright on her own for awhile. Or don't you know how to dance?'

Embarrassed, he rose quickly, and followed her out onto the floor. The music was soft and slow now, an old tune not of the band's own composition. Angie danced well, and Jim was beginning to feel the effect of three swift pints on an empty stomach; his feet felt light in their new dress shoes, assured and agile, unable to do harm. They'd switched off the strobe and slow arcs of green, red, yellow and blue now swam across the floor and over the faces of the patrons who stood with their backs against the bar. He liked the feel of his palms against Angie's body, the way her blouse shifted beneath them as she moved. The music was still loud enough to make conversation difficult; Angie had to lean against him and speak into his ear, chatting about pop groups and videos, the best places in town to go for a meal. He closed his eyes and listened to her, answering with an ease that surprised him when she paused. He had a sudden vision of their getting married, of settling down with her, providing for the children she would bear him, looking after her and them as they all grew older and the demands on their time together became less strident and mundane. The set ended, and when Angie hugged him he clasped her to him tightly, not wanting to let go.

She smiled up at him, her chin resting lightly against his chest. 'Well. That was really nice.'

'No, wait a minute,' he said, catching her arm as she turned away. 'You'll break it.' Somehow her necklace had snagged on one of his buttons; he squinted at the knot in the uneven light but he couldn't see where it began.

'I guess we're attached,' she joked as the band returned to its previous volume and the strobe light again began to spin. The floor filled quickly as the music gained momentum; the two of them moved gingerly step by step until they were standing in a steady beam, then studied the problem as best they could while couples and trios of lovers and friends twisted and swung around them.

'Can you unbutton it?' she shouted above the din.

'No, it'll just go through the hole. How about you, can you undo it?'

''Fraid not; you've got the clasp in there.' She pointed to the knot.

They looked at each other sheepishly for a minute, the floor throbbing beneath them. Across the room Denise was dancing with a small, thin man whose gaze was fixed on his shoes.

'What's up?' she mouthed, dancing towards them, her partner trailing awkwardly by her side. Angie pointed first to Jim's shirt and then to her necklace, made a tugging gesture with both fists and shook her head ruefully in reply. Denise's laughter could be heard above the band.

'Nice one!' she called to Jim as she moved back into the crowd. 'Very nice!'

'Never mind her,' Angie said loudly. 'What do you want to do?'

'I think I've almost got it,' he shouted back, struggling with the fraying thread which held the button in place. The sudden snap jerked them apart; the button came off and the chain unravelled smoothly of its own accord. Abruptly the band switched to a faster beat, and Jim grabbed Angie's hand and pulled her towards the bar.

'Good thing your mummy hadn't mended that yet,' she teased him as he paid for their drinks.

'Here! I do me own mending, thanks very much.' He took a quick gulp of beer and wiped his lips on his hand. Angie was straightening the small bends the knot had put in her chain, and his own fingers ached to brush the hair from her face. 'I'm good about the house,' he ventured recklessly. 'And I like kids.' In the dim light of the dance hall he wasn't sure if she blushed.

She excused herself and followed after Denise, who was waiting for her at the far end of the bar. She took Angie's arm and bent towards her ear; Jim saw her answer with an embarrassed smile, shaking her head without conviction and only half-shrugging the question off. He drained his pint and ordered another, feeling warm and happy. Gib had been right about the Abercorn. He gazed fondly at the people around him, wondering why he and Fitz hadn't come here more often instead of wasting their time in the pubs on the Road. He hadn't realised how tired he'd been of their familiar faces – all the girls he'd grown up and gone out with for ages. It was so good to get out, to meet other people. He felt rich and magnanimous, buoyed by a tenderness which could embrace all humanity. He chuckled softly; Gib would've told him it was only the beer.

'What?' Angie asked as she moved in beside him. She'd put her hand on his shoulder climbing onto the barstool, and the small gesture of intimacy made him swell with pride.

'Nothing,' he said. 'Just thinking, that's all.'

'What about?'

About the way you looked coming towards me just now, he almost told her. No other girl seemed nearly as pretty. There was something about Angie that made everything easy, and abruptly he wondered if she were Born Again; the one or two other people he knew who had that same power to affect those around them were all recently Saved. Even Denise was less brassy around her. The blonde would be good for Gibbons, Jim decided; she was as mad as he was but she'd still calm him down. He pictured the six of them a few years from now in a new-smelling car, he and Angie, Fitz and his girl, Gib and Denise, ordinary married couples with their children on their way to the seaside for a bank holiday weekend.

'How's the necklace?' he asked instead.

'Oh fine,' she said. 'I'm always doing something like that – breaking things, knocking things over. The first time I wear a new dress I always spill something on it. True confessions,' she said sheepishly.

Jim laughed, risked patting her arm. 'Is that all?' he said heartily. 'I can beat that.' And he told her how to this day he couldn't do laundry, how he'd flooded the kitchen the last time he'd tried. Somehow they got on to curiosities – she told him her ankles were double-jointed, he showed her what he could do with his ears. She said a cousin of hers could crack his knuckles indefinitely, and her sister could fit her whole fist in her mouth if she tried; he had a friend who'd lost all his baby teeth and never grown any back. He must have wasted his wishes, she said, and that got them exchanging superstitions – point at a cemetery and your finger'll drop off, hold your breath crossing bridges and you'll never drown, never let a lamppost split you off from a friend or you and that person'll fall out before you get home.

'See a pin and let it lie, to good luck you'll say good-bye.'

'That's only for the day, but,' he answered. 'Crack a mirror. That lasts seven years.'

'Spill salt,' she countered. 'That's bad luck, too – I don't know for how long.'

Jim searched his memory for an effective rebuttal, but his brain was addled. Someone had bought a round for the bar, and the shot he'd ordered was taking effect.

'Rosemary beads,' he announced finally.

'Rosary beads,' Angie told him. 'What about them?'

'If you break the string the pieces'll bleed.' She looked at him sharply. 'That's what they tell me,' he said hastily, 'I wouldn't know myself. Right enough,' he went on, more to himself than to her, 'we used to steal them off the girls from Our Lady of Mercy when we were kids, and they never bled for us.' The memory made him chuckle. All that kind of carry on seemed so long ago now.

'Well,' Angie said, 'thanks for the drink. I'd best be off.'

She was on her feet already, and the sudden change in her stature took him by surprise. 'Ah, c'mon, it's still early, isn't it?

You don't have to go yet.' He struggled up from his seat and reached for her hand. She pulled away.

'Here, don't get me wrong about them rosemary beads,' he said anxiously, 'I didn't mean nothin by it.'

She stood in front of him silently, her eyes on the floor. That she didn't struggle or pull away again was encouraging, at least, and he tried to come up with something else that would make her want to stay.

'Tell us about being a Christian,' he urged. Again she looked at him as if he must be mad. 'I'm not winding you up,' he promised her, hoping he'd sound sincere. He felt himself roll on a wave of panic, a physical sense of the urgency of the moment which made caution seem cowardly.

'Just, don't go,' he said. 'Please.'

'Look, I'm sorry you got the wrong idea about me.' She paused, apparently struggling over what to say next. Anxious to reassure her, he shook his head.

'Okay, so you're not a Christian; it doesn't matter. Sure, there's worse things than not being Christian.' Like being Chinese, he told himself silently. The thought made him grin.

She stepped back, resolute. 'Look,' she said, 'I really have to go.'

He watched her push her way through the dancers till she found Denise. They spoke together briefly, then the blonde glanced over at him, her expression hard. The music stopped while the band changed instruments, and for a moment he lost sight of them in the crowd. By the time the view cleared Angie was gone; Denise had collected their coats and was headed towards the door. On the stairwell she stopped, stabbed two fingers in his direction and appeared to spit on the floor. Then she, too, was gone.

His throat felt dry, so he signalled the barman, but when the pint came the look of it put him off. Since he'd paid for it, he drank it, feeling his belly expand as he did. When time was called he realised it was later than he'd imagined, and he suddenly felt weary, drained by a fatigue that was more than physical. He found his jacket and went down the stairs to the street.

The weather had grown steadily worse while he'd been inside. He pulled his collar around his throat and peered up at the sky, wondering whether to run for it or wait till the rain died down. But then two men and a woman came out of the club, and as the entry wasn't big enough to protect them all he decided he might as well move on.

He ran to the end of the street, his head down against the wind, but the barricades were up and he couldn't get through. The rain had disoriented him; he couldn't remember which way to turn for Royal Avenue, and without people the narrow streets of the city centre were unwelcoming, the cold, iron faces of the shop fronts anonymous and severe. He blundered about for a good quarter hour, coming up against one locked security gate after another, before he finally stumbled across a main street and spotted the row of black taxis ahead.

He ran straight to the first car in the queue; Silverstream, Springmartin, Glencairn – any one of them would take him up the Shankill, and from there he could easily walk home. There were three other men already in the back and a woman in the front; Jim pulled down the seat behind the driver and sighed. What a night, he thought. I should've saved the money and stayed at home.

The driver tossed an empty crisp packet from his window and switched the cabin light out before pulling away from the curb. In the dark, lulled by the hum and gentle massage of the engine, Jim allowed himself to relax as best he could. The man opposite him was large, and had made no effort to make room for him when he'd gotten in. The other two, his age, were long and lanky; they'd stretched their legs back out as soon as Jim had entered, and the one by the door had his feet up on the empty seat. Jim closed his eyes, intrigued by his body's readiness for sleep. His mother would have saved him something – a sandwich from supper, maybe a few chips; there might even be enough hot water left for him to have a bath before he went to bed. Tomorrow, or rather, today, was Sunday; he could go round to Fitzy's in the afternoon and let him in on the crack. He'd get a laugh out of it, anyway. See, Jim? he'd say. You're still crap with women, even without us around.

The taxi lurched suddenly over the broken road, jostling its occupants and dislodging the feet from the seat beside Jim. Their owner swore and lifted them stiffly back up again, nursing his shin. His companion laughed.

'Still sore, eh?'

The other shook his head darkly. 'Too bloody right.'

'I told you she was wild, son,' the first one said with some satisfaction, 'but would you listen to me?'

Jim smiled; it was good to know that other men were apparently having women troubles at the same time he was having his. The big man pinched the ash from the end of his cigarette and dropped the butt in his pocket.

'What happened to him?' he asked the boy beside him.

'He was in a fight,' the other said. His companion muttered something vicious under his breath which the first boy ignored. 'If she'd been any taller she'd've really done some damage.'

'Bloody women,' the big man remarked without venom.

The statement had a universality about it which Jim could appreciate. Unable to catch the big man's attention, he gave what he hoped to be a wry smile to the boy next to him.

'What she kick him for?' the big man asked.

The other shrugged. 'It's his own fault. He was keepin her goin.'

His companion looked up from his knee. 'Is it my fault she can't take a joke, the stupid cow?' he demanded defensively. 'It's not my bloody fault.'

'Now, now. I told you what she was like, son. But would you listen?'

The big man grunted. 'They're all like that,' he said, 'bloody women. There's no point talkin to them. You want to talk, talk to your mates.'

The boy beside him nodded with the expression of one who has just heard his own opinions on a subject stated succinctly by an expert in the field. His friend placed his foot gingerly on the floor of the cab with an exasperated sigh.

'It's not my bloody fault,' he repeated sullenly. 'Silly cow. We should've gotten that carry out.'

'That's what I said,' Jim laughed. He'd been waiting for an opportunity to make some contribution on the other boy's behalf. Women were unpredictable; it didn't seem fair to argue that a man should have known better than to say whatever he said that upset them so.

The other boy looked up gratefully. 'You too, eh? What happened to you?'

Jim grinned. 'Well, she didn't kick me, anyway.'

The boy laughed. 'Where was this?'

'The Abercorn.'

'Oh, aye. Good place for girls.'

Jim grimaced. 'Don't know about that, now. I suppose it's better than the Road. But…' There was a general murmur of agreement. 'Still,' he continued, warming to the topic, 'there's good crack in the Rex on a Saturday night. Live music and all – country and western, mostly. The Three Amigos.'

The others looked at him curiously. The big man retrieved his butt and struck a fresh match on his shoe. The flame shed a disk of yellow light against his chin, and for a moment while he cupped it his hands hung disembodied, their image mirrored in the glass beside his head.

'Where'd you say you go, son?' the big man asked, dropping the match on the floor.

'The Rex,' Jim repeated amiably, 'just above Agnes Street.'

The others said nothing. The boy by the door lifted both legs back onto the seat opposite him and folded his arms across his chest. The big man drew heavily on his cigarette and settled back in his seat, his eyes on Jim's face. Suddenly self-conscious, Jim looked out at the road. It was strange the way the streets and houses lost all identity in the rain. Running around like a lost sheep in the city centre had been disconcerting; he knew the town like the back of his hand, it wasn't like him to lose his way. Again he thought of Angie, and he felt his guts twist. Too much to drink, he decided. I'm going to have to cut down.

Through the window he watched the rows of terraced houses flow by, their outlines blurred by the thin film of rainwater wobbling over the pane. They passed a kebab house, and the sight of it made him hungry; if the weather had been any better he would have gotten off there, bought himself a chip and curry, and walked the rest of the way home.

He was falling asleep when the taxi finally slowed and pulled into the curb. The door opened and a man climbed in, pulling a duffel bag in behind him. He exchanged a terse greeting with the man opposite Jim and nodded to the other two. Then the light went out and the taxi drew away.

The big man cleared his throat. 'How was it?' he asked.

'Fine, fine,' the other said.

'Did youse win today?'

The other grunted. 'We never do.'

'Bloody hurley,' the big man sympathised, and the other silently agreed.

Casually, so as not to draw attention to himself, Jim turned to face the window. He could see shops now, some with their shutters down, a few others standing empty, their windows smashed, their signs removed. On the gables of the houses that rubbed shoulders with the road he could see the murals, shadows of gunmen, weapons, flags. His throat dry, Jim turned round to the driver.

'Next stop, mate.'

A silence had fallen over the men in the back of the cab. Jim continued to watch the road over the driver's shoulder, but he could feel the others' eyes upon him. The woman in the passenger seat shifted uncomfortably, readying her money in anticipation of getting out. As he slowed to a stop, the driver switched on the overhead light to take the coins from her and make her change. Still searching for his own money, Jim twisted towards the window between the front and back parts of the cab, but it was closed and he had to wait for the woman to put her purse away and gather her bags. She climbed out and slammed the door behind her; then the driver switched the light out and once more pulled away.

'Here, wait a minute,' Jim said, 'I'm gettin off.'

The taxi gathered speed. Jim's hands were cold; he curled his fingers into his palms to warm them but the chill that had plagued him since he'd left the club had settled in his bones. Outside, the rows of dark and silent council houses swept past, their blinds and curtains drawn. The road had grown wider and was rising above the estates on either side, the buildings below black and uniform, falling ever farther away from the kerb. His eyes smarting, nearly blinded by tears, Jim turned away from the window and folded his arms, waiting for it to be over.

Inheritance

I N MY MIND I have always remembered Mandy's sixth birthday
as the day my mother began her affair with Big John
Trowbridge, at six-foot-seven the tallest man any of us had
ever seen. He had come to Belfast from America like so many
others, to volunteer in the west of the city and observe the war at
first hand. It would have been easier if he had been somehow
different from the rest, from those who came for a year, maybe
two, and then went home to their families or their educations, got
on with their year of travel or returned to their proper jobs. But
he was not different. He was an ordinary man of indeterminate
qualifications, remarkable only for his silence and his stature,
who was neither good nor bad with children. Compared against
all others, he was a youth worker of indifferent talent. If we did
not love him, we tolerated his presence, and in deference to his
size accepted his authority as Craft Room Supervisor in the
House.

The House was semi-detached with four bedrooms, the last in
a row of terraced public dwellings. So poorly had it been
constructed that it had been scheduled for demolition almost
from the day it had been built. Though it had never been resi-
dential, now and again a volunteer arrived whose personality was
of sufficient strength to assert itself above all others. In this way
the House had been known as Jill's, then Edgert's, then Henri's,
then Oskar's, each individual imparting the faint flavour of his
native land through his name until some other came to take his

place. Ostensibly the House still belonged to the same church which once had hoped to fashion it as a small, unofficial head-quarters for local youth evangelism, though these efforts had been without success. Gradually we had taken it over, until in the end we had cemented its reputation as an unruly, ill-managed community youth club. Complaints were lodged with the Housing Executive that the House had become a haven for alcohol and solvent abusers of all descriptions, yet still it survived every attempt to close it down. Quietly, then, and with few regrets, the church had disavowed all public connection with the House; privately, however, it still channeled a few pound per week towards its upkeep, and continued to solicit the services of foreign volunteers in the hopes that they might preserve some semblance of respectability until the Executive finally did tear it down.

Too young for the pubs or for sex, too poor for the leisure centres, the bookmaker's, or the off-licence, we had nowhere else to go, and would have come to the House had it offered its four bare walls and nothing more. At the very top there was a Reading Room, but as there was nothing more to read in it than what we ourselves had written on the walls, we used it for tumbling and wrestling matches whenever we were allowed inside. Downstairs there was the Games Room, with an aging snooker table and a dart board, pockmarked and cratered with abuse, but this room was often closed to us deliberately, as punishment for articles stolen the previous day. On the rationale that the House was ours and that its contents therefore belonged to whomever among us was able to take them, we stole everything we could fit in our pockets without being seen. The TV and Disco Rooms on the ground floor had fallen victim to theft so often that virtually nothing remained in them to distinguish them for what they were. Just the television itself was left, too large and bulky to be carried away but inoperable nevertheless, for some industrious individual among us had at some point stolen the plug.

Only the Craft Room never failed us. Although it was small and poorly lit, it was a peaceful place, strangely sheltered from the arguments and uncontrolled activity on the floors below. Though its shelves and cupboards were sparsely stocked, the little they contained – stiff reams of gold paper, tubes of glitter, rolls of discarded Christmas wrap, nearly new; all the small implements for the making of crafts – fascinated us, and we were always eager for the few hours a week Big John let us inside.

He was invariably punctual, and usually the first of the volunteers to arrive, appearing no later than five minutes to three. From on top of the broken wall at the far end of the street we would wait to see him round the corner, some ten to fifteen of us, often having queued from half past the previous hour and clinging to the stone and plaster which crumbled like cheese and came away in our hands. Though we fixed ourselves to him like leeches, he could have been anyone come to open that door and we would have been as enthusiastic. Upstairs in the Craft Room, we would scramble and fight for a seat at the long table. Big John sat not at the head but at the centre of that table, and each week while we worked produced a new object for our duplication in the weeks that followed: toy boats from lolly-sticks or baby dolls from clothes pins or tiny play houses from old egg cartons and bits of cloth. He never spoke to us while he worked, though we were never silent. We chattered on around him endlessly, but our narratives provoked no greater response than a slight deepening of his soft, faintly critical smile. He was twenty-eight when he came to us; he was just past thirty when he left, and yet throughout his stay he remained aloof, detached, deliberately distancing himself from the situation into which he had chosen to come. It was as if he had sacrificed something by coming, had martyred himself emotionally or professionally, and daily struggled to suppress the contempt he felt for us all. The story went round that he could have been something had he only stayed at home, a doctor, perhaps, or even a judge, or he might have come into a fortune and been a millionaire had not some unknown set of circumstances forced him to come away.

Though the House itself was open every Monday through Thursday, Big John opened the Craft Room only once a week, on Wednesdays from half past three until ten at night. When the new estate was completed, we'd been placed in a house just ten minutes away, yet despite the insignificant distance involved, my mother, weak-kneed from reading the *Mirror* and the *Sun,* insisted that we be escorted both to and from the House once evening settled in. Someone would call to collect us, she promised, and we were not to leave the premises until that someone did.

At first my father had said he'd do it, he had nothing better to do since he'd been made redundant eighteen months before. And he did do it, regularly and without enthusiasm, just as he'd done his work in the shipyard before they'd let him go. But soon the layoffs came like contagion across the whole estate, and then he no longer had to suffer the humiliation of watching the telly alone in the house for hours on end with no better company than that of his wife and the women of the Road. Instead he joined the ranks swollen by the men of his own age and station with whom he had grown up, and ten days after Mandy turned six he took up his pint and his place among them intside the door of the Crown.

My mother had planned a party for Mandy's birthday. It was to be a small affair, but it would have been the first party she had given, for a child or for anyone else, and she'd spent weeks planning it. I'd discovered her clipping coupons and digging out the tinsel and other Christmas trimmings two months after they'd been put away, but as usual I took no notice. She was forever rearranging furniture and redecorating rooms, always subjecting us to unusual recipes and exotic foods, forever dying and cutting and restyling her hair. These eccentric overhauls occurred so often that Mandy and I had come to follow our father's example and pay her no heed, whatever she did to her person or our home.

In the end, as she must have known he would, my father said we had no money for such things, and sure, a child of six didn't need a party. My mother had been like a train derailed, and in anger had answered too sharply. He spoke sharply in return and raised his fist, and though he did not strike her she cried for hours all the same. Having expected no celebration neither Mandy nor I was disappointed when none was forthcoming, and so my mother was left alone with her loss, waiting for the summer and a fortnight's holiday with relations in Strabane. Using the rift as an excuse for his absence, my father would leave for the pub as soon as it opened, and because he would not appear again until after it had closed, my mother began collecting us for our tea.

The first night my mother came for us she stood at the bottom of the stairs and called, telling us to hurry before the meal turned cold. Ten minutes passed and still we ignored her. She'd grown impatient waiting downstairs in the open doorway, self-conscious and shivering in her summer cardigan and slippers, shy in front of the volunteers. They were men and women her own age yet they looked much younger, young people without the facial pallor brought on by an early marriage and children arriving before the ring. Go on up yourself, they told her when again she called us and still we did not appear. Go on up, they urged, have a look around.

It's been over ten years since that evening and still I regret whatever childish prank or preoccupation kept me from seeing my mother's face that first time she saw him. I imagine her arriving short of breath and irritable at the top of the stairs and seeing him sitting there, head bent over a pot of yellow paint, surrounded by children so much smaller than himself, two of them hers by another man. I would have liked to have seen if she loved him immediately, if her face flushed with the unexpectedness of it all, if her breath had gone gasping from her throat when she saw him, if her hand had reached out to steady herself from the fall of falling in love. My father and his family have always told me that what happened was an ugly thing, and all too expected from a woman who was never satisfied. They said she'd always been that kind of woman, and a drinker, long before their marriage, long before the dole and debt and his own drinking could take the blame for anything at all. But still, I should have liked to have seen.

Despite her eccentricities, my mother's was the voice of law and order in our home. It was not that our father was weak; he was merely indifferent, a natural state of existence only accentuated by unemployment. His role, as he saw it, was to sire his children and keep us all fed, if not with a wage packet then with a benefit cheque. Now and again he issued sanctions against what he perceived to be the overexpenditure of money. But he had nothing to say about the state of his house as long as it was as clean as his mother's. He cared little for the progress of his children's education, social or intellectual, so long as their names did not appear in the local papers and were not part of the evening news. It did not matter to him that publicity could be a mark of achievement as well as a disgrace. Once, when our class had taken top honours in some scholastic endeavour and I had shown him the picture of me in the paper, bright-faced with hair unbrushed and leaning too far forward over the girl in front, he'd dismissed my success with the grim prediction that I'd soon be sorry I'd won. Why couldn't I be like the other girls from the Road, he'd asked, and thus avoid their envy? As for his wife, he cared less still, just so long as she remained his.

Consequently it fell to my mother to deal with any requests for pocket money and all permission slips from school in need of a signature. It was also she who meted out punishment, regardless of the nature of the offence. For all I would have muttered and Mandy would have cried, had she commanded us to come home even once in those first few weeks we would have gone. But she did not, and gradually some adult part of me recognised the pretext for what it was. After that first encounter, she would arrive at the House early every Wednesday, sometimes as much as two hours ahead of time, and come directly up the stairs to the Craft Room whether we were up there or not. There she would sit like a truant schoolgirl, her eyes brightly coloured above her lashes, her lips slightly parted and pinkened thickly before she'd left home.

At first she did not realise that she could spend time with him only on Wednesdays. The Thursday following the day they met I took the day off from school. From my parents' bed where I always lay when ill, I listened with eyes shut tight as my father left with Mandy shortly after eight, waking only much later to the sound of her singing and the watery rush of the tub being filled. Through the gap where the wall did not quite meet the ceiling came the scent of bath cubes crumbled over warm water, carried on a heavy, porous mist which clung to the windows and to the surface of everything in the room. For an hour the thickness of it cushioned me more gently than the duvet and pillows on which I lay. Then came the harsh, choking rasp of waste water draining, and I heard the sound of her towelling, a hazy, static noise amidst the soft click and clatter of bottles replaced and the soap dish recovered. When she came in a few minutes later, robed and turbaned and scented like a queen, I watched her, mesmerised by the methodical recon-struction of her outdoor face and hair. When she left more than three hours after she had begun I still had no idea where she was going, but I do know I pleased her when she twirled in front of me and I answered her, Aye, you are looking well.

She was back quite quickly with Mandy in tow, her face, like the child's, streaked with angry, indignant tears. She must have entered the House with some breezy greeting ('Hullo, just here for the children'), leaving herself with no other choice, when she did not find him there, than to simply take her daughter and go. For the next few weeks she made disparaging remarks whenever possible about the state of the House and the character of the volunteers employed there. She repeatedly questioned the level of discipline and even threatened to call the Health Board and demand that the place be closed down.

I suppose now that she must have blamed him for his absence, held him responsible for the embarrassment and humiliation of her mistake. But at the time the motivation for her behaviour was a mystery to me. In fact, so convincing was her performance that Mandy and I sincerely believed that we'd soon be prohibited from attending the House altogether. Gradually, however, she did recover and was full of praise once more for the work we brought home and for those who had helped us with it. Aloud and within my father's hearing she began to remind herself to spend more time with us in the House. Considering how much time we spent there, she'd say, she'd hardly see her children if she didn't. And my father, dismissively, would agree.

I can recall quite clearly the image of her sitting, a woman over thirty, spending hours painting pictures of simple square houses, big-headed flowers, and smiling yellow suns like a child of six or seven. At thirteen the only cure I could find for the sharp twitch of embarrassment I experienced whenever I saw her was to ignore her completely, and I taught Mandy to do the same.

But it was a lesson my sister learned better than I. I tried not to look at them; I even tried to avoid them, to concentrate my attention on activities taking place in some other part of the House, but I could not. My mother's fascination with Big John fascinated me. On those afternoons when the Craft Room was closed I'd loiter downstairs and watch him play chess with the Over-Fourteens, studying his face as he studied the board, considering the length and shape of his fingers, the varying shades of his moustache and beard, but so much did my mother's performance disgust me I could see nothing attractive about him at all. At night and on weekends when my father was home I'd catch myself staring at him the same way, unable to penetrate what it was about what made them different that could effect a difference in the way she behaved.

That no one else commented upon it or even appeared to notice how doggedly she pursued him was baffling. That children younger than myself and lacking the family connection should be oblivious did not surprise me, but I was convinced that the volunteers were more astute. My mother would inevitably be the last to leave at the end of the day, dallying with an air of studied distraction as she collected her belongings and apologetically summoned her children, who were usually already waiting for her downstairs. On one such occasion, eager to complete some project or another, I too had remained after the hour but still found myself impatiently urging her out ahead of me. Big John was standing in the doorway, holding it open, his usual signal that the room should be cleared. As my mother crossed the threshold he reached out abruptly and flicked on the light above the stairs. The gesture drew her up short; she stepped back and I stumbled into her from behind. I looked up irritably from whatever crushed creation I had been holding just in time to catch the warmth of the smile she flashed him, and the bold way she looked directly into his eyes. Perhaps she was flattered; no one had ever lit her path or held a door open for her before. She went down the stairs then, past some other volunteer on his way up, and I saw the look the two exchanged behind her back – Big John with his eyes towards heaven, the other's suggestive, sympathetic grin. I imagined them talking about us after we'd left and laughing at my mother's affectations, and I resolved to have no part of her from then on.

For a time she tried to discipline us while we were together in the House, to play more a big sister's role than a mother's, but eventually she found this too distracting and gave up on it altogether. When she was away from him she sat in debilitated silence, poking the coals or staring out the window; most evenings she parked, open-mouthed and vacuous, in front of the TV. For six days out of seven she was listless and depressed, yet so trite was the image she conjured that something inside me sneered even then. I could feel no empathy, no understanding for her at all. Perhaps as a consequence, I no longer feared her, and was soon challenging her authority even outside the House.

More than any murmur of gossip, it was this change in our behaviour towards her that first roused my father's suspicions. Stay in, she'd say, and we'd go out; leave that, she'd tell us, and we'd cover whatever it was in palm prints and smudges, so determined were we to do the exact opposite of whatever she decreed. My father, distracted from his track lists or the television by an unusually flippant bit of cheek (which, like all others, went by unchecked), would watch her watching nothing, her eyes vacant but never dull. With what appeared to be clinical detachment, he observed the gradual decline in my performance at school and Mandy's sudden, unprecedented reputation as a 'difficult' child. To him such developments were merely a part of growing up; he expected a child's bad behaviour to be directly proportional to its size, and children were bound to lose interest in schoolwork, just as one might lose an old mitten or a mismatched sock – such things could always be replaced by something better. But when my mother failed to draw his attention to or even pass comment upon these changes, he began to wonder why.

He was not alone. After an unrewarding stretch during which they periodically quizzed both Mandy and myself and sent notes home with us which we invariably destroyed, a barrage of teachers-cum-social-workers eventually appeared in person on our doorstep to enquire if everything was 'alright' at home.

Had it not been for their involvement, we might well have gone on indefinitely as we were. Though something had certainly changed, whatever it was had had virtually no effect on our day-to-day routine. The house continued to be cleaned, albeit with less energy. My father's meals continued to be ready whenever he required them, and he was not the kind of man to notice a decline in the aesthetic quality of his food. And if his children had grown somewhat more wild than they had been before, at least they were no more poorly behaved than any other on the Road.

But my father hated any intrusion into his privacy; he hated the

false solicitations of strangers and their hesitant, obtrusive prob-
ing into what he devoutly believed to be none of their business.
To his mind there could be no validity to their protestations of
mere friendly concern. Because they called round on a
Wednesday, my father, who only by accident was in to receive
them, was caught disastrously off guard, and endured the ensu-
ing interview in visible discomfort. Though he offered them tea
and sent a boy round for chocolate biscuits while it brewed, he
was unprepared for such domesticity and bitterly resented
having been placed in a situation where he could not help but feel
a fool.

For they could not have chosen a worse time to call. Whether
for fighting or spitting or using profanity, I'd been sent home early
from the House and had taken Mandy with me when I went. But
my mother, blinded and deafened and struck stupid by love, had
failed to register the fact of our departure and so remained behind
on her own in the Craft Room with the other children and Big
John, leaving my father to explain her absence to the two quietly
observant faces who had come to call. Oh, is she a volunteer with
the community house, then, Mr Millar? they asked, and I watched
his face flush with anger and shame as he lied.

He did not tell my mother of the Social Service's concern for
her family's welfare; he did not tell anyone, but still she learned
of it from the Road. So pervasive appeared the communal knowl-
edge that my father began to find it difficult to pass his associates
outside the wine lodge, let alone go on inside. His pride was
dependent on appearances and on what others thought of him; it
did not well up from any source within. Had they called him a
cuckold, he would have hung his head and believed, just as he
had when he'd been told he was unemployable, that he was too
old for night school, that he was 'too Belfast' and would never fit
in overseas.

My father had never been a particularly inquisitive man, let
alone a demonstrative one. He preferred to suffer most things in

silence or ignore them completely rather than confront them head on. But these encounters with his peers annoyed him. He knew they ridiculed him for allowing his wife to indulge in any antics whatsoever, however innocent. To curtail her involvement with other men was, after all, the reason he'd married her. And so he decided to revisit the House.

On the day my father came, Big John had set most of us the task of tearing strips of newspaper from the vast outdated pile in the corner of the room. He positioned those remaining round an old porcelain wash basin and from a safe distance directed us in the creation of a crude papier-mâché mixed from flour, water, and powdered glue. Though we had been given a plastic spoon and the broken handle of a brush with which to mix it, these tools were soon discarded in favour of the more efficient if less tidy method of simply using our hands. Big John, intrigued, perhaps, by the pleasure it gave us, plunged his own hands beneath the murky, oatmeal-coloured waters and caught momentarily at our groping fingers, pulling them down still deeper into the cool, trembling gel that had settled at the bottom. My mother, who had been primly cutting paper with a pair of blunt-tipped scissors, now joined in enthusiastically, squealing in mock horror whenever someone's hand grabbed hers. When my father appeared in the Craft Room door to claim his wife and children, she was up to her elbows in wet newsprint and paste, her new frock speckled with flecks of white flour, her nose still wrinkled and her lips still pursed in distaste from the moment before when, at some child's urging, she had gingerly tasted the glue.

Considering its potential, it was a disappointing moment. Silence did not fall upon us; the general chatter and splash continued uninterrupted. No one stared, no one passed comment; my father made no accusation and my mother expressed no surprise. Instead, he spoke only her name when he saw her, and she came to him like a dog, or like one in a trance, immediately and without protest.

Had she not behaved so meekly at that moment, had she not exhibited such cringing humility but had instead told him that in all the time they spent together she had never so much as touched this other man and whenever she addressed him she always called him Sir – but she told him nothing. Had I been older and less likely to be spiteful, I could have been her witness and her ally, and perhaps I would have been believed. After all, when I was not in the House I was just in front of or inside our own, and so was she. She could not have managed to slip away unnoticed, and she never offered any pretext to get away. Nor was she the kind of woman who would fondle her lover in the local community house in full view of children. Once, at her request, when I'd shown her my textbook on Greek mythology and she'd seen the picture of naked Perseus, she'd flushed like a virgin and hastily turned the page. But because she would not defend herself, I assumed, as did my father and everyone else on the Road, that the rumours were true, that she must have been guilty of something, that perhaps she'd even gone to him or let him come to her as soon as her children had left for school.

Within days my father'd left her. He took us with him when he went, an unusual decision for a youngish man without a job. He'd have crossed a body of water to keep her from him, or so he said, and I suppose he did, in a small sort of way, when he crossed the Lagan to the other side of town. But after five days of his brother's whining, his sister's refusal to cook for or clean up after him, and his parents' tremulous demands upon his time and money, he decided to bring us back home.

The house was empty when we returned. Just as he had gone to his mother, so she had sought shelter with hers, returning to the same small room whose yellow curtains and Pierrot clown decor had remained unchanged and waiting for just such an emergency since the day she had left thirteen years before. In later years my father's family blamed her even for that, claiming hers was the easier move, her mother being bright and healthy and having no other responsibilities that might have distracted her from the care and support of her daughter. For two weeks nothing was washed; we ate no breakfast, had school lunches for dinner and various take-aways for supper and tea. He could drink more easily with his friends at the pub but when he came home he could not sleep – and still his pride would not allow him to speak of her, let alone go after her and ask her to come back. Then one afternoon she simply reappeared, and because he did not acknowledge her presence one way or the other, she put her things away in their bedroom up the stairs and did not leave again.

They remained together for another three years, until my father joined the army and went to serve overseas. Mandy and I stopped visiting the House, and eventually a combination of arsonists and vandals closed it down. With admirable opportunism, the church organised a complete philosophical overhaul of its mission in the community and reopened a more overtly Christian rendition of the House in another part of town, but by then Big John had returned to America. He never wrote back to us, not to the House or the volunteers, not to the church which had employed him, or to me when I sent a query at the age of seventeen demanding to know the truth. Perhaps he had been her lover, but it didn't seem likely; perhaps he had no idea what part he'd played in the episode at all. I meant to ask him the day he left from Aldergrove, and arranged to go along with a small crowd from the old House with that purpose in my mind. The party had been organised to send him off, to see him board the big, bright plane that would take him home and make sure that he got away without complication or distress. But there were delays on the motorway, an accident or an incident, I don't remember which; and when at last we arrived at the airport he was already gone.

Rise

———

THIS IS A list of the things that went missing: half a metre of green nylon netting, a small quantity of stainless-steel gauze, a bolt of cheesecloth, two pairs of forceps, eight sheets of plywood and a box of syringes, half a dozen light bulbs, a spool of wire, a fret saw, a hammer, and a packet of needles.

It's that boy, my uncle Vincent said. What did I tell you about that boy?

Now hold on a minute, my father said.

Hold on, nothing, my uncle answered. That's who's done it. And it's your own fault for taking in strays.

Alright, we'll go see him, my father said, but when we got to the house he wouldn't go in. Instead he went up to a man in his shirt-sleeves who was leaning in a doorway on the other side of the street. The man straightened up when he saw us coming, and the girl on her knees in the hallway behind him sat back on her heels and set her brush down.

Michael Hagan, my father said. D'you know if he's in?

He is, the girl said. He's been in for a week.

He's sick, the man said.

Why, what's wrong with him?

That woman's what's wrong with him, the girl said. She took a sponge from the bucket beside her and slapped it down heavily onto the floor. Good bloody riddance if she has gone away.

They don't know what's wrong with him, the man said. He took sick last Sunday and he's been bad ever since.

Is it serious?

Could be, the man said. His mother's with him. A couple of

times now she's sent for the priest.

A bad time to visit, then.

No, go on over, the girl said. She'll be glad of the company. It's been ten days now and he's not said a thing.

In the kitchen of the house we found a woman standing, her back towards us, making tea. Steam climbed from the mouth of the lidless kettle, but the woman's grip on its handle was bare. There were cakes on the table, a pile of cores and torn strips of peeling half-wrapped in newspaper on the edge of the sink, and the room was rich with the scent of cinnamon, the air just above the open oven still quivering with escaping heat.

Mrs Hagan? my father said, and she turned.

Yes?

How is he?

Just the same. No change from this morning.

Is he eating?

Not a thing. I just took him soup but he wouldn't touch it. I tried porridge earlier but he left that, too.

And what about you, how are you doing?

Oh I'm alright, the woman said. I'm bearing up.

Have you sent for a doctor?

The woman looked at my father, at his tie and his spectacles, at the pen in his pocket and the briefcase in his hand.

Aren't you the doctor?

No, my father said, no. Just a friend.

From inside the cardboard box he carried came the fluttering sound of confetti falling, of raffle stubs tumbling before the draw. He offered the box like an explanation, and all of a sudden the woman's face cleared.

Oh, aye, sorry, she said. I do know you. You're the one who got him that job.

She led us up a narrow staircase, assisting each step with both hands on the rail. The woman's ankles were as thick as her calves, and I could hear the quick, uneven clouds of her breathing escape from her open mouth as she climbed.

That was awful good of you, she said on the landing. He liked that wee job.

Eight months before when my father found him – legs wide apart and fists on the table, staring down at a tray full of Bull's Eyes and Moon Moths my father had pinned the previous week – the jimmy he'd used to lever our window was in his back pocket, and the sack he'd brought to put things in was lying still empty at his feet. So what do you think of the royal family? he'd asked without warning. My father had spent the past forty-eight hours on a bench outside of Intensive Care; he'd stared at the boy in the black leather jacket, at his close-shaven head and the tattoos on his arms – trying to distinguish the uneven letters, to see in the purples and blues of the symbols an emblem he recognised, a slogan he'd heard – and said nothing. *Citheroniidae,* the boy had continued, they come from America. Only they're lumped in with the Saturnids now. Reclassified, my father had answered. That's right, the boy'd said. Seems they were silkworms, after all.

Michael, you have visitors, the woman said.

He was in a wooden chair by the window, and he didn't look up when we came in. Every flat surface – most of the floor, the desk and the dresser, the low wooden unit beside the bed – was cluttered with field guides and uncut labels, specimens in transparent envelopes, others on spreading boards, a few behind glass. My mind formed the names of the ones I could recognise – *Colias hyale,* the Pale Clouded Yellow, its wings and antennae outlined in lavender; *Lysandra coridon,* the Chalk Hill Blue; *Callophrys rubi,* the Green Hairstreak, fringed from wing tip to thorax in the softest of greys.

You should see it downstairs, the woman said. The kitchen's full of them. I couldn't believe my own eyes. Every drawer and closet in this house, every shelf, full of them, and not one crumb of food in sight. Just those things, everywhere.

We've brought him another one, I'm afraid, my father said. He handed the cardboard box to me. Go on, wee woman, you give it to him. He'll like it better, coming from you.

We had brought him a new imago, the first to complete the cycle that started with the eggs we'd discovered in the field Michael introduced to my father, one of the few laying patches he hadn't yet found. What do you look for? my father'd asked him. All morning they'd been comparing notes. Michael shrugged. Videos, mostly. TVs, if they're small. This was shortly before my father hired him, paying him out of his own benefit cheque. Sometimes Michael would let me help him, let me pass a pin through the tight coiled centre of a slender proboscis and draw it down into sugar water till the insect stopped struggling and started to feed. The trick was to see if we could get them all started before the first one finished and began to walk away, wings open- ing and closing with the tentative speed of untried machinery, taxiing slowly in preparation for flight. We'd managed it once, working together, till all around the room on greaseproof paper Apollos and Peacocks and Camberwell Beauties were swallow- ing nectar, while I watched their wing patterns shifting and thought about bedsheets with people underneath. Don't move, Michael said when the last one had finished and I'd just returned it to the breeding cage. His hand brushed my cheek as he reached past me, and I expected to see a string of silk handkerchieves, or the smooth removal of an egg from my ear. Close your eyes, Michael told me, and I'd felt its feet flailing, frantically scrambling to re-establish their grip; then its claws caught my skin with the tug of small anchors, and I thought of moored ships and hot air balloons in extravagant colours, tethered and straining against their cords. You can look now, Michael said, and there it was, a Great Spangled Fritillary, indignantly fanning, imagining itself bold and imposing when every tremor of its rust-coloured wings sent another shower of scales to my palm.

Look, Michael, I said.

It had made its way into an upper corner, had been testing the meeting of lid and wall there, when I opened the box. Placing one slender leg carefully after another until all six were pinching the rim, it climbed out, broad head first and wide-spaced antennae, then the short, stout body, wings flat at its sides – a butterfly, despite all the evidence, though even its flight was quick and erratic like a moth's. I felt the effort of its ascension just as I had when, with my father, I'd been a passenger in the plane he'd hired for an hour as a gift for my mother, who had always wanted to learn how to fly. We'd stood by the fence which guarded the runway, watching other aircraft take off and land while the pilot pulled levers and adjusted dials and untied the cords that kept our plane bound. They all seemed to rise with the smooth, steady lift of geese leaving water; I'd never imagined the shuddering fuselage, the thrust and drag of my heart and stomach, or the way my own equilibrium wavered with each changing attitude of the plane. The land below us looked artificial, like the scenes behind glass in the museum at home, tiny figures of farmers and livestock grazing on velvet under parsley sprig trees: *Belfast and Surrounding Country, 1790–1801.* It bore no resemblance to what we'd seen of it when we'd taken the highway a few days before. We had come out of season, long after harvest, and well before blossoms hid the hunched, arthritic fingers of the peach trees again. The wizened phalanges of the apple orchards, the electrified carpals of the cherry trees we passed, the charred spinal columns of the naked vineyards, each with its singular pelvic twist – I could almost hear the startled hiss of them when our headlights swung round a corner and caught them unawares. Ah, look, my father'd said, slowing the car, and gradually my eyes did catch sight of them: Canada geese, two only at first, then three, then five, then a dozen or more, a whole flock of throats and bills and bandaged white jaws rising out of the mud and stubble of a cornfield in April in upstate New York. We'd intended to spend the day in Toronto, but Immigration had refused to let us in – something to do with our type of visa – so we were skirting the rim of Lake Ontario, hoping to see Canada on the opposite shore. But the weather was wet, and the lake barely visible; I could feel the mist on my face when we got out of the car – cool, like my mother's breath on my back as she slept behind me, all three of us together in a motel's queen-sized bed, and gentle, like the trick Michael taught me soon after she died. Give us your hand, he'd said, bending down, till I felt something lighter behind the touch of his hair, the insistance of eyelashes against my arm. Do you know what that is, missus? he'd said. That's what you call a butterfly kiss.

You see how it is, the woman said to my father. I've tried to get him to talk about it but he won't, at least not to me.

You don't know what's happened, then?

Not all of it, no, but I can guess. You know she'd gotten a job in England? Well, I thought she was fixing it so he'd have work, too. Three months go by and every day I'm thinking, He'll be off soon now, too, but then I hear she's home for a visit. I never saw her myself, but I know she saw him. The couple next door says she stayed for an hour, went away in a taxi and that was it. Then the milk bottles and papers started piling up. They knocked on the door but nobody answered. That's when they reckoned they'd better ring me.

I had no idea, my father said.

No, well, how could you? Sure he never said anything to anybody. She's found herself some fancy man, that's what I think, anyway. I don't know what she told him, but he's been like this ever since.

It's been awhile since we've seen him, right enough, my father said. But the weather's been nice, you know? I thought he might be collecting. See, what did I tell your Uncle Vincent? My brother-in-law thought he'd been stealing again.

It wouldn't surprise me, the woman said. But he's not been out of this room for a fortnight. Was it stuff of yours, aye? You're welcome to look for it. I couldn't tell you what's in this house.

No, my father said, I'm sure it's not Michael. It's been going on for awhile, see. A couple of things disappear every day. I think it's me, to be honest. I misplace things. I don't know what I'm doing half the time anymore.

Well have a look anyway, the woman said. Sure, I'll make us a wee cup of tea while you do.

Thank you, my father said. You stay with Michael, daughter, alright? he told me. Try to get him to talk. I won't be long.

He was wearing pyjamas, his arms loose in the sleeves, each elbow at rest on an arm of the chair, and still I could see the inflated vessels altering the contours of his forearms and hands. I took hold of his wrist and turned it over, placed my two fingers at the heart of his palm and began to move up with a circular motion, crossing thin strands which began in confusion and later became conspicuous cords like the gradual gathering of slow drops of water, each bead jumping to join the stream till a single clear thread runs briefly down the length of a windshield or the cool face of a window, drains itself utterly and then is gone. Michael had taught me the game only recently, and the first time we'd played I'd fallen right into the trap, saying Now! There, stop! when his fingers were still a good two inches away from that tender hollow where an arm bends in, where the skin is creased even in infants, thin and defenceless behind the elbow's sharp bones. It's because of the way the nerves are laid out, Michael'd told me. It always feels like you've touched it before you do. But this time my fingers were well past the hollow and on toward that place near the armpit where all flesh turns smooth, in men as in women, regardless of age. I walked my two fingers onto his shoulder but he never responded, so I lay his hand back in its former position and smoothed his sleeves down.

You're awful pale, Michael, I said.

My mother had been white when the plane landed. She'd been sick for more than a year already, which is why my father had borrowed from usurers despite unemployment and the impossibility of ever paying them back, so she could visit her brother who now lived in America, having immigrated from Belfast some fifteen years before. But this time the illness refused to resettle, and a few days later we'd had to go home. What does it feel like, I'd asked her in hospital. Like you felt at Funderland last summer, she'd said – when I'd made myself sick on the main attraction, the one that replaced the Big Wheel that year. I forget the name of the ride now, but not the sensation. It began with the rise and tilt of the axis, then the floor fell away as we started to spin, the centrifugal force of lopsided rotation kept us pinned to the sides of the iron cylinder, the crush of the wind came from all directions, and against every warning I had opened my eyes. The bright colours of the cars and pedestrians on the Lisburn Road, of the shop fronts with their fruit stalls and displays of appliances, nearly new clothing and secondhand books, all tumbled towards me as if someone had lifted the asphalt at Shaftsbury Square and shook everything down towards the spot where I hung, the only solid the boy strapped opposite me, his own eyes shut across the bottomless space. I turned my head to look for my parents, standing by the ticket booth on the good ground below, and the skin of my face stretched tight as elastic, my flesh seemed to pass through the metal grille, and I thought of wax melting, of the disintegration of the Lundy's features that time on the Shankill when I'd watched him burn. I'd gone on a dare with a boy from Clonard Gardens, had stood at the end of a row of old houses and watched the flames consume the effigy, thinking, How much wasted effort. I had an art teacher once who made models and drawings for illustration, to show us precisely why our own projects failed. With broad thumbs and fingers he'd bend and pinch the mysterious clay, or with quick charcoal sketches of femurs and vertebrae, he'd illustrate the error which had crippled our plan. When he'd finished he'd destroy the model or scratch out the drawing and say, Now you do it. I'd often wondered how that point could be reached, when I'd no longer be invested in every project, when a torn sketch wouldn't trouble me, when I could watch easily as they dismantled my armatures, as the screws were recycled, the wire unwound.

How do you feel, Michael? I asked, but he didn't answer. I followed his gaze out the open window, down the drainpipe at the edge of the sill to the patch of waste ground beside the house, where someone had dumped an old pot of tulips and some other horticultural rubbish in a tangle of weedroots and unwanted leaves. The lepidopterans of the floral world, my father once called them, and then tried to explain it to my cousin and me, how at every stage in a tulip's development it's transformed completely, how the final blossoming of the chaste, contoured petals was like the first full extension of a butterfly's wings. We'd spent the day looking for Painted Ladies, waist-deep and oblivious in the lush fluidity of the grass, and had come upon an inexplicable row of the flowers, paint-box bright, aloof and unblemished, in a rain-rutted pasture in County Down. The leaves look like cow's tongues, my cousin said, to be clever, though I could see the connection if I tried. I remembered a cow my uncle was supposed to have slaughtered; the animal had given him all kinds of trouble when he tried to drive it onto the truck. My uncle's cows were in Niagara County, on land which he left in the care of a neighbouring farmer a few months after we visited him there, so he and his wife and his son who was my age could be with us after my mother died. The cow's knees had been trembling badly and halfway up the ramp it'd balked, so three men were enlisted to help push it in. They stood side by side with their hands on its haunches, but their boots slid backwards over the gravel and damp diamonds of sweat appeared on their backs and under each arm. When they did finally get it into the back of the pickup, had pulled the ramp away and were raising the door, the cow's eyes turned white, its legs buckled beneath it, its tongue rolled out like a jubilee carpet, and the hard knob on its head where its horns would have been made the chassis ring as it fell.

I don't understand it, my uncle'd said. She was great yesterday. The beast wants to live, Vincent, my mother'd said. Well if it does, my uncle'd answered, that's a strange way to show it. But he did phone the abattoir to say the cow was unhealthy – and that was the reason he kept on giving whenever the subject of slaughter came up, though every morning when we went out to look at her she was grazing serenely, her coat sleek, her belly enormous, her ears and eyes and hindquarters imperturbable, despite the relentless assault of flies.

Any luck? my father asked from the doorway.

I shook my head.

No, I wouldn't've thought so, the woman said. It's alright, luv. Don't you worry. He'll be right as rain again in a couple of days.

Listen, Mrs. Hagan, my father said, if there's anything I can do, you'll tell me, won't you?

What can anyone do? the woman answered. These things happen.

Well, if there is anything, you let me know.

You can catch that thing again, the woman said. It's over there.

The Skipper had landed on a heavy curtain which hung in front of the closet instead of a door. My father approached cautiously, assessing the distance, then removed his coat to improve his reach, but still his hand missed its target. The Skipper flashed once and vanished, then flashed again higher up; the half dozen tacks which had held the curtain popped like snaps on a raincoat and I heard their soft tinkle as they hit the floor, then the room overflowed with Sulphur and Brimstone, Magnificent Julias, True Lover's Knots. They came to rest on my sleeves like the dead skin of a bonfire, light and unsteady and easily dislodged – all the ones my father couldn't sell to collectors, all the ones whom the opposite gender ignored, all the outcasts who for some reason had hung incorrectly after eclosion and so had been unable to inflate their wings fully or straighten their legs before the cuticle grew hard. Their flight made the sound of old wooden houses alone in the country, their floorboards and panelling resisting strong wind, and so many of them flew at my face on their way to the window that I had to close my eyes.

When I opened them again I looked for my father. He'd knelt down beside Michael, had the boy's hands in his, and they both were watching the steady exodus as even the most crippled among them struggled onto the sill and fell out, towards the light.

The Swing of Things

Y OU GO ANSWER it, my father said when the doorbell rang. I was up to my elbows in lemon bubbles, a butcher's apron around my waist, but he took the pot and scrubber off me and held a clean towel while I dried my hands. Go on, luv, he said. I'll finish these.

Brian and Jack were my honorary uncles, and though I'd just seen them the previous evening they still hugged me close when I opened the door, the scent of cologne fresh on their collars, their cheeks newly shaven and smooth against mine. My father came from the kitchen and stood behind us with folded arms.

Is he ready? Brian asked me, before he saw him. I ordered a taxi.

I'm not going, my father said.

You are, Jack said.

Now look, said Brian, we've been through this already. He unbuttoned his coat with determination and aimed his voice at the other room. You don't mind, do you, Mr Scully?

Of course he doesn't, Jack said. He went over to where the old man sat in his chair by the fire and crouched down in front of him, eye-to-eye. Alright, Grandad? he said. What's the forecast?

There's too many chickens, the old man said.

So there are, Jack said, straightening up, I've always said so. See – what d'I tell you? Sharp as a tack.

For God's sake, said my father. Can't you see I can't go?

Listen, comrade, Jack said, it's not immigration; it's one night on the town. We'll have you back here within twenty-four hours.

I don't know, said my father. What about the child?

She's a good big girl, aren't you, luv? How old are you now? Seventeen? Twenty-one?

She's nine, my father said. Too young to be left in the house on her own.

But she's not on her own, Brian said, she's with her granda. You'll look after her, won't you, Mr Scully?

He's got to get out, the old man answered, but my father shook his head.

He doesn't know what he's saying. That's not about this.

He knows more than you do, Brian told him. They looked at each other in silence for a moment. C'mon, now, Brian said finally. You'll be in by midnight, earlier if you want. And you don't have to do a damn thing you don't want to, alright? Just get out of the house for once, that's all, have a few pints and watch the match.

My father sighed. Who d'you say's playing?

Liverpool, Jack said. And this time they'll win.

For the next twenty minutes they stood beside him in the downstairs toilet watching his razor move in the mirror, lifting their chins with the same squint and pout as he scraped the blade carefully across his throat. Then they followed him up to the back bedroom to help him match a clean shirt and tie, where they shook out his suit and condemned its condition, spit-polished his shoes, and vetoed his socks until my father gave up and let them choose a pair. I heard them arguing about financial matters – who'd pay for the pints and the grub if they got any, how much to save for the cab fare home – until my father came in for his jacket and cap and the spare set of keys, kissed the old man on the top of his head, and said, Alright, luv, I suppose we're away.

A man was closing our front gate behind him when we stepped outside looking up, testing the odds in the blush of clouds above us of another summer evening ending in rain.

Hiya, the man said, and shook hands with Brian because he was the closest. Gus Holden. Is one of you a John Scully? I was told

I could find him at this address.

Is that right? said Jack.

What for? Brian said.

Your name's not Holden, my father said. You're a McCulla. Pascal McCulla, from the Ligoniel Road.

Not any more, the man said. I've been Gus Holden for ten years now.

Your father owned a sweetie shop when I was a boy, my father continued. Remember, Brian? Across from the post office, near Leroy Street. How's he doing, your dad? Does he still have that shop?

No, no, it burned down years ago. He and my ma live in England now.

McCulla's a good name, Brian said. Why'd you change it?

Part of the job, the man said. You do what they tell you or you don't get paid.

Listen, Pascal, my father said, John Scully's my father, but he's not very well; I don't like to disturb him. Can I help you at all?

The thing is, the man said, it's your da won the prize. I don't think it's transferrable.

Jack shook his head like a man clearing water.

He's done what did you say?

He won a prize, the man repeated uncertainly. He was in a competition. He won a day out with me.

And who are you?

I do stunts, the man answered. He seemed embarrassed. For the cinema, mostly. Sometimes just for show.

What kind of stunts?

Lots of things. Get set on fire, jump off of buildings. The usual stuff.

That's not true, Brian said. You do that thing with the catapult, don't you? Off an eighty-foot bridge with a plane going by. You catch hold of it. I saw it on TV.

Yes, that's right, the man said. But I do the other stuff, too.

You should see that one, Brian said generally. That's really something.

It's a bit late for a day out, isn't it? my father said. It's almost seven now.

Aye, I know, the man said. But youse aren't on the phone, and I have a cousin in Velsheda Park I haven't seen for a while, so I reckoned I'd stop by here first and make plans for tomorrow or whatever day suits.

Jesus, Jack said. How about that.

A competition, my father repeated. What kind of competition? What did he have to do to win?

Oh, I don't know, said the stuntman. Just be a fan, I suppose.

No offence, Jack said, but that's just not possible. You sure you have the right address?

It says John Scully here, right enough, Brian answered, examining the letter the stuntman had taken from inside his coat. And it's your street and number. He refolded the letter and returned it, shrugged and shook his head. Looks like it's him.

Have a look in his room, Jack suggested. He might have the rule sheet or something up there.

No, said my father, he's got to have privacy. This is his house, too, after all.

So what do you want to do? Brian asked quietly.

We were on our way out, see, Jack told the stuntman.

Oh sorry! he said. I can come back tomorrow.

You're here now, Jack said. Hold on – you wouldn't mind staying here for a while, would you? Just for a couple of hours, to keep an eye on things. You'd be doing us a real favour, letting this fella have a night out for a change. He grinned at the stuntman and patted his back. Don't worry; you'll understand everything when you've met the old man.

Now wait a minute, my father protested, that's not on.

What about your cousin? Jack asked, ignoring him. Is she expecting you?

No, not at all. She doesn't know I've arrived.

Well that's it, then! Jack said. We'll be down at the Joxer for a couple of pints. They're showing the match on the big screen. You can see it yourself, if you want to. He's got a TV.

I don't feel good about this, my father said.

Don't be silly, Brian said, it's a great idea. As long as you don't mind, of course.

It's alright, the stuntman said, really. I don't mind.

When they were gone I led him inside. The old man was sitting just as I'd left him, and I went over and collected his plate from the table beside him and removed the napkin from his lap. His fingers shook as I wiped them clean.

What's all this for? said the stuntman, looking round him.

For him, I explained, so he doesn't get lost.

I'd written the first set myself, one for every door in the house. But bright colours confused him so my father made new ones, simple black letters on white, unlined card – one to say TOILET, another, COAT CLOSET, the three bedrooms upstairs identified by occupant, the back of both exits reading, THIS LEADS OUTSIDE. In our kitchen too everything was labelled. A note on the breadbasket reminded the old man where to find butter, another on the kettle told him how to make tea. TURN THIS OFF! said a sign on the cooker. My father had changed it over to electric after he found the old man still looking for matches an hour after he'd switched on the gas. The following week he'd stepped through the gate the postman had left open and struck out for Carnmoney, where he used to live. He'd gotten as far as the city centre, had even managed to find the right bus, but the coins in his pocket had made no sense to him, and though he'd lived all his life within a twelve-mile radius he was disoriented completely when the driver pulled away. He'd entered a shop but lost sight of the exit, had drawn the attention of a security guard, then stood in front of the Linen Hall Library counting the same fifty-pence piece over and over until the thought of the sum he believed he was carrying had paralysed him with dread. A whole afternoon of pedestrian traffic had moved him gradually to the opposite side of Donegall Square, where Brian walked into him on his way home from work. From then on we kept the gate bolted beyond comprehension, and he carried a card on his person printed in large letters with his name and address.

I checked the carriage clock on the mantel, stoked the fire, and switched on the pump.

It's time for his bath, I told the stuntman. Do you want to come up?

We followed the same procedure each evening. The first thing was to sit him down on the toilet, get his clothes off, and then fill the tub. I'm going to unbutton your shirt now, Da, my father would tell him while I got the old man's toothbrush ready and tested the water against my wrist – Lift your feet up now, let's pull off those socks. After the bath there were ointments to use for poor circulation and swollen joints, plus an assortment of tablets and liquids which had to be taken before going to bed.

I took everything off him but his vest and pants, then I opened my mouth so he'd open his and pulled my lips back in the grimace necessary for the brushing of teeth. My father shaved him every morning but by teatime his chin bristled against my palm, the short white stubble on his jowls sparkling like frost in the bright light of the bathroom.

I don't think they cleaned it, he said as I wiped his lips. It's gone now, anyway. Audrey, luv, did I give you that one? There was something else the last time, you tell him. Did he take that one away with him, too?

Okay, I said, stand up a minute. I fastened a towel around his waist, reached up underneath it and pulled down his briefs. As he stepped into the bathtub I took the towel away and helped him sit down, and when he let go of the handrails I lifted his arms up and pulled off his shirt.

Aren't you going to answer him? the stuntman asked me.

No, I said, he's not talking to me. It's your hair, I explained. Audrey's my mother. She used to wear hers that way, too.

Hers had been thicker than his, however, and even longer, and when she tied it behind her the dark strands moved in lazy unison, like the tail of a horse. Who do I look like? I'd asked her one evening when my father and I were sitting beside her, one on either edge of the bed. We were looking through a shoebox of photos he'd come upon earlier while searching the closets for something to have ready for Mrs Mercer, who collected donations on behalf of the church. Like your father, she'd answered promptly, but he'd disagreed. He'd lifted the soft rope of hair from her pillow and tousled his own head next to mine. Look at that colour, he'd said, there's your answer. You see that, wee girl? You're a bit of us both.

The stuntman examined the ends of his own hair curiously, as if he'd only just realised how long they'd grown. I gave him the soap to hold so I wouldn't lose it, and the shampoo to pour when the time came for that.

Listen, he said, can he go outside?

I recalled the forecast, the violet horizon, the mild breath of the evening on me as I'd waved Brian and Jack and my father goodbye.

I think so, I said. But not for too long.

It's just that he did win this competition, the stuntman continued. He deserves something for it. There's got to be something outside I could do.

I dressed the old man in the clothes my father had already set out for him to wear the next day, a combination of garments he'd been fond of once. To be on the safe side I put a cardigan on him, then I led him downstairs and out into the garden where the stuntman stood, contemplating the house.

He was in his bare feet and he'd taken his shirt off. White gauze bound him from midwaist to abdomen, swift movement seemed difficult, and I don't know why but I thought of my father, whom

I'd happened to see once stepping into the bath. The door to the bathroom had been slightly open and I'd caught a thick glimpse of flank and buttock before he sank in, lifted the sponge from the water beside him and squeezed its load slowly over his head; all the strength with which he'd been fooling us drained away from him then. Some time before that I'd observed the woman who lived across from us step into her garden perfectly nude. Her body was a nest of soft folds and deflations, like those of the models who posed for night classes in Life Drawing and Sculpture in the art room at school. The first time I saw them disrobe with such confidence and then mount the platform to pass the interminable hours outstretched on cushions or strad-dling a chair, I'd been with friends – we'd just finished Swimmers, and waiting for someone to come fetch us home we were wander-ing the corridors, intrigued by all that the building was home to after school hours, independent of us. From then on I watched regularly the Adult Ed students seated at easels, the hesitant strokes of their pencils and chalk, the thoughtful perambulations of the silent instructor and the all the while oblivious expression of whatever naked man or woman was in front of them that week. The old man had recently moved in with us then, my mother had only a few months to live, and I already had doubts about my own body, already imagined I could see proof of its impermanence in my own face and limbs. The woman's husband, returning from work as she stepped from the house, had dropped the plastic box he was carrying which still held his crusts and wrappers from lunch. He'd put his arms around her and held her, and it occurred to me then that this is why we fall in love: because we need another's eyes to convince us we remain things of beauty, because without another's tongue to tell us we assume such words can not be said.

The stuntman touched his bandages gently.

Bad back, he told the old man as if he owed him an apology. It's going to catch up to me one of these days.

How'd you get it? I asked.

I'm not sure, to be honest. The littlest thing can cause an injury. Bobby Dunn knocked an eye out doing a high dive – there was a match on the surface and he hit it coming in. I've been doing a lot lately with airplanes and ladders; that kind of thing can throw your spine out of whack.

He carried a chair out from the kitchen and I had him put it where the old man could see, then he excused himself and returned to his survey, tugging briefly at the drainpipe, gauging the likely strength of the gutters, testing the soundness of the moulding and quoins.

I don't know, he confessed finally. I haven't done anything like this in ages. Everything's so high tech these days. I used to work a lot with animals, too, but I hardly do anything like that now. That's how I got started, actually – training horses in Connemara. The first film I did was with Peter O'Toole.

Sargano wrestled lions, the old man said, Bostock boxed with kangaroos.

The stuntman stared at him. That's right, he said. So they did.

I put money on the barber, the old man went on. I'd've liked to've been there. Your uncle, he was living in Lancashire, he wrote me about it, but it wasn't the same.

Not Tom Helme, the stuntman said cautiously, but the old man was plucking at the cuffs on his cardigan and didn't respond. Helme shaved a man in a cage with six lions, the stuntman told me, must be forty, fifty years ago now. He was a barber; he did it on a dare.

So what do you think? I enquired at length. He'd inspected the house now from every direction, and I'd seen him eyeing the distance to the roof of the garage from one of the windows on the second floor. By now dusk had dulled the edges of everything, and although his fingers were as warm as ever still I worried about the old man.

I could make up a rig if I had some boxes, the stuntman offered.

There's a Spar round the corner, I told him. You might find boxes there.

I'd need a lot of them, but, he said, his eyes on our chimney. That drop's thirty foot if it's an inch.

There weren't enough but he took what was there. A cardboard wall rose quickly in front of him, its layers compact and orderly, printed with CORNFLAKES, WHITE CLOUD and ARIEL AUTOMATIC. He found the old sheets my father had used to cover the furniture when preparing a room for the old man's arrival; the cotton still smelled of turps and was stiff as rubber where the paint had congealed. He threw these over the boxes and bound it all loosely with twine.

Don't try this at home, he said when he'd finished, then climbed easily up the drainpipe onto the short roof of our scullery, turned, and sat down.

Not to worry, he said. When I first started out I worked with this fella who used to say there's no such thing as a more dangerous stunt. That was true then, it still is, a little, but there are some stunts now that're more easy than others.

They told him he was finished, never lift'm again, the old man said. In some places they were half an inch deep.

Jesus, the stuntman said. Dick Grace. Now he was one of the greats. Outlived eighteen professional rivals; another four had to quit cuz of injury. He was a mess himself after that accident, right enough – 786 square inches, burned so badly his arms ended up webbed to his sides – but he cut the scar tissue with a razor so he could keep on working. It was him used to talk about outwitting gravity. The stuntman laughed softly, then shook his head. Jesus, he was fearless. It just didn't trouble him, the thought he might die.

When I was much smaller my mother told me that should we ever be separated in a shop or department store I was to stand by an exit, and she would come and look for me there. You still remember that? she'd said when I reminded her of it – though I suppose, she'd added, it's not so long ago. She'd been weak, however, and a doctor was coming, so I never did explain the reason I mentioned it – the conclusion I'd come to regarding death. The way I see death, I had wanted to tell her, it's a circular room in which I'm at the centre, and though I fight hard through the people to get to a wall, though I travel along it and feel for a door, the same faces keep passing with the slow regularity of unclaimed luggage, and I end up repeatedly where I began. But no other opportunity ever presented itself, and later I realised what I'd been describing was not death at all, but the waiting room outside it where all the rest of us are.

That's madness, I said.

The stuntman shrugged. We have to go sometime. I suppose he reckoned with the end coming at him it'd do him no harm to meet it halfway.

He stood up. I heard the sound of scuttling gravel, a clump of moss dislodged from our shingles fell swiftly past and vanished into a flower bed, then I spotted his head and shoulders, his elbows cocked on either side, and in an instant he'd levered himself over and was coming towards us across the roof of the house.

It's okay, he called down from the edge. The rig's a wee bit smaller than I'd like it, but you can fall fifty feet on dry land without damage if you know what you're doing. He crossed his arms over his breastbone, his fingers clasping the back of his neck. Backwards and sideways, he explained over his shoulder, and spread-eagled on impact. That's the safest way, usually, for this kind of thing.

He described the mathematics of arcs and projectiles, the various forces that determine a fall, but all I understood of what he was saying was the margin of error, something they'd tried to teach us in school. An explosion in town the previous evening had damaged a gas main near the building, and as we were already facing evacuation we'd gone on a field trip to the Ulster Museum to see an exhibit on the concept of chance. The rest of the group moved on without me while I lingered at one of the first displays, an upright contraption of transparent plastic through which a torrent of ball-bearings perpetually bounced down from a single opening into a row of compartments below. Though their descent was described by the force of gravity, it was the force of their knocking against the short, even pegs which were there to obstruct them that shunted them into a bell-shaped curve – and I thought as I watched them repeating the pattern how everything in life was this accidental. Despite all the care of the hands that place us, trying to centre us so we fall just right, still our paths remain unpredictable, we're so easily sent veering by a single peg – success, disaster, and recovery all equally uncontrollable, whatever the odds and calculations.

All set below? the stuntman said.

Out of sight around the corner I heard our gate hum.

All set, I answered. The stuntman nodded and stepped back with long strides, disappearing in sections from the bottom up. Then my father was beside me, our front door key ready between his fingers.

I thought I heard your voice, he said. What are you two doing out here? He touched the old man's forehead with the back of his hand. Are you alright, Da? he demanded. Where's Pascal?

Again the gate groaned and shuddered. My father, glancing back to see who was coming, said Ah, no, and shook his head.

Now, what did you think? Brian replied before he could say anything.

I told you, my father said. I just wasn't up for it. Why didn't youse stay there, enjoy the match?

Who needs football when there's home entertainment? Jack answered. Just in time, by the look of it. Have a look up there.

It seemed he spun from the edge in slow motion, off by many inches and almost certain to miss the rig, and I thought of the way glass shatters, the regal burst of liquids when they land. The cord around the boxes snapped when he struck them, the sheets leaped up with the sound of someone heavy elbowed out of slumber into turning over in bed, and flattened bits of cardboard shot out from under, scattering leaves and twigs. Grit and plaster pattered softly on the bushes as the pieces stopped revolving and slowly came to rest.

Jack was the first to reach him. He pulled the sheets and cardboard away like a man in a hurry rifling through drawers while my father and Brian followed behind him, stepping gingerly into the path he'd cleared. What I saw first when they finally reached him was the stuntman's chest heaving, the careful way he drew up his knees.

Easy, now, my father said urgently – Hold on! Don't move.

I'm alright, the stuntman said, sitting up. A thin strip of bandage grew taut behind him and he stopped abruptly.

Just wait a minute for God's sake! Brian said. We'll ring for an ambulance. There's a hospital just down the road.

It's okay, the stuntman said, I feel fine. With an effort he stood and brushed the dust from his trousers. Miscellaneous joints clattered irritably as he stretched.

You are one daft bastard, Jack told him with admiration.

C'mon inside, my father said. I don't care what you say – you ought to have someone look you over.

I'm alright! the stuntman insisted. But I could do with a drink.

Good idea, Jack said, we'll go to the local. I'd very much like to buy this man a Bass.

Not me, thanks, said my father, youse three go. I want to get that child to bed. Da? he called, and they all turned with him to look back at us. You okay?

The old man had risen when the stuntman fell. The last time I'd seen him move so quickly I'd been much younger and spending the day with him at his house. A year before that he'd tackled the bare, uneven land that lay behind him and created a pond, and I was keen to see proof of what he'd told me, that from the first bucket of silver he'd spilled into the water had come a whole population of healthy fish. We'd approached the bank quietly but still the pond's rhythms had been disturbed; it was many minutes before they returned. There he is, he'd whispered finally, pointing to the source of that retching bellow whose tremor I'd felt in my own throat and chest. He'd eased himself off the log on which we'd been sitting, I saw his arm strike with a heron's speed, and all at once he was crouching beside me, his shirtfront splattered, the frog with its large golden eyes and vulnerable belly afraid but uninjured between his hands.

I put my hand on the old man's shoulder. He said, You're a good girl, Audrey, and placed his hand over mine.

We're alright, I answered. We're okay.

Punching In

THE HOUSE WAS one of the older models, three up, two down, with a toilet outside. They'd had little to put in it when they first moved in; they'd had less still eighteen months later. She'd had no jewelry to pawn, no silver or china, no family heirlooms, no antiques. He had a watch but he wouldn't part with it. Neither one of them would have considered selling the TV. So when the time came when there was no food in the house and no money to buy more, she'd sold all but the two sets of cutlery, two plates, two bowls, two mugs for tea, and a saucepan, and told herself she never intended to entertain.

They'd been together off and on for more than seven years; they'd been married for close to five. During that time he'd gone with other women, been done for reckless driving and accused of assault, stolen from her handbag, and hidden the money from his benefit cheques; only rarely did he manage to hold down a job. Why the hell don't you leave him, Maureen? her sister would ask when they met in the town. Who else'd have me? she'd always say. It was easier to make a joke of it than try to explain.

She had known him all her life, first as children and then in school. She'd taken up with him almost by accident; they'd ended up together at a party once, had been out a few times after that with a crowd, until gradually they were assumed to be a couple, and a rumour had surfaced that they were engaged. She'd had a few other boyfriends when she was younger, but eventually the need to earn money had taken them away, one to England, another to America; one had left and come back again, but by then he was married with a family of his own. She'd seen that one again recently, with his wife and daughter, when they came into Belfast for the christening. Albert had sent her to the shop for fags, and she'd run into them outside the church on the way. She'd declined their offer to attend the reception, cooed at the infant, and tried to hurry on, but the wife had detained her, chatting about Canada and asking Maureen what her husband had been like as a boy. She'd had a terrible time getting away.

Maureen stood now in the queue at the corner shop remembering the encounter. That one and his wife had seemed happy enough, and she'd been happy for them; she didn't know why she'd been so unsettled, why she'd felt the need to stop in a cafe for a quick cup of tea when she could just as easily have made one at home. She'd given no thought, until she'd been asked, to the pale, silent boy who'd held onto her tightly on those few occasions they'd gone out on the town, whose features still lingered on the face of the man whose thumb had been locked in the child's firm grip, who had recently stood with his wife who was not from Northern Ireland and agreed to the price of a new house in Bangor. When Maureen did get in, Albert was waiting at the foot of the stairs, angry this time because she had lingered and had made him miss the start of the match. Their own TV wasn't working – he'd broken the plug tripping over the lead – and he'd been planning to watch the game down at the pub. He'd hit with such force that the front door had splintered at the hinges, and she had to call the Housing Executive to get the thing repaired. For a week it hung half open; when the repairmen finally arrived they told her the frame itself was shattered and would have to be replaced. Sometime next week, missus, they told her, when she asked them how long that would be. Then they removed the door and went away.

'What're you after, luv?'

The woman across the counter was large and in bad temper, the shop busy and she on her own. A full mug of tea and a half-eaten pastry had clearly been sitting by the till for some time. Maureen felt a knot of panic draw tight in her chest, as if those behind her had suddenly surged forward and clamoured to be served.

'Two pickled onion, a pint of milk and a quarter of cheese, twenty John Players, and a packet of Homewheat, please.'

'We don't do biscuits now, luv,' the woman said irritably. 'Just the singles: Penguins, Clubs, Breakaways...'

'Give us two Fruit Club, well,' Maureen said quickly.

The woman's glance was sour. 'No Fruit, just Milk or Plain.'

'Whatever then, it doesn't matter, either one.'

'Plain?' the woman demanded, reaching up among the boxes and bottles of sweets arranged in dusty rows above her. Maureen nodded.

'That's okay. Whatever.'

The woman let her arm fall heavily to her side and turned around.

'Which do you want, luv? Milk or Plain? C'mon now, there's other people wantin served.'

'Plain,' Maureen said. 'Two Plain'll do nicely.'

She paid for the items and left the shop. The weather was fine for the time of year, and the Road was crowded with children, pensioners, and women with prams conversing on street corners and outside of shops, all obliviously obstructing the uneven flow of pedestrian traffic. Maureen stood for a moment blinking in the sun, checking the mathematics of her purchase in her head.

'Mrs Reid? It is Mrs Reid, isn't it?'

Maureen turned swiftly at the close sound of the voice and her purchases fell to the ground along with her change. A young man in a clean white shirt and a girl in a pink suit stood before her. The girl was holding a diet cola, a scone, a small tub of yoghurt, and a green apple, all neatly but unstably stacked against her blouse; the man held a sandwich in a cellophane box. Both were smiling.

'Mrs Reid,' the young man said. 'I'm so glad I caught up with you. We've been trying to get hold of you for weeks.'

Maureen stared at him blankly. His face and voice were vaguely familiar – and she thought of the envelope that had arrived that morning, the latest of a number addressed to Albert, who'd opened it without interest and waved her away. She bent quickly to retrieve her belongings, conscious of their eyes on her as she knelt. From where she crouched she could see that the girl's stockings were sheer and fashionable; a delicate line of small flowers climbed up from each ankle and disappeared beneath her skirt, and for a moment Maureen imagined her as she might have been when she bought them, consulting with a girlfriend about the colour, the new suit with which to match it off-the-rack fresh and heavy on her arm. Then she caught sight of the young man's shoes, so brightly polished she could see the hazy outline of her own reflection.

'Here, let me help you with that,' he said as she stood up. He tucked the sandwich under his arm and held out his hands expectantly, but there was really nothing for him to take or do.

'It's alright,' Maureen said, holding her purchases closer. 'I've got them, thanks.'

'Look, it's nearly two – your appointment's for quarter past, isn't it? If you're free we could go over to the office now, have you out for two-thirty, what do you say?'

The girl beside him opened her mouth then shut it again, her lips thin.

'I've got your file, the new forms, all the stuff since last year,' he continued. 'Haven't you been getting our letters? Everything's just been waiting for you.'

Maureen shook her head dumbly, casting about for any excuse, conscious that he was waiting for an answer.

'I couldn't possibly,' she said, 'not right now – '

'It'll only take a moment, Mrs Reid. It's best to get these things out of the way. If you take care of it now you'll have less trouble later.' He turned to the girl and flashed her a grin. 'We'll have lunch tomorrow,' he told her, 'I promise – my treat.'

The girl's shoulders fell back into place; her lips relaxed their pout. She gave Maureen an expressionless smile then turned and headed back up the Road.

'But my husband,' Maureen protested. They were standing on the kerb just inches from the traffic, the young man gazing easily in both directions with her elbow in his grasp. Maureen looked up into his smooth, unblemished face. 'My husband,' she said again, raising her voice as he hurried her across, 'he's waitin on me.'

He guided her past the small streets and entries which branched off from the Road, chatting on about unemployment and entitlement, her outdated claim for Housing Benefit and how this had been altered by Income Support. Just outside the Social Services building he let go of her arm and shooed her in front of him, followed her onto the lift that stood waiting and tapped the button for the second floor. Maureen felt her stomach fall away as they rose.

'This'll only take a moment, Mrs Reid,' the young man repeated, examining the contents of his sandwich with a critical eye. When the doors parted, he propelled her lightly towards a small man with thick glasses, engrossed in a battered tabloid from the previous day. The air above him was blue with cigarette smoke, the window at his side discoloured with its stain, and Maureen wondered where his gaze would wander when he'd finished with the paper and had nothing left to read. He noted the time from a thick, strapless watch which lay face up on his desk, scribbled briefly, and handed Maureen a small numbered form. Then she and the young man passed on behind him, through a set of swinging doors.

On the far side of the large airless room that they'd entered, where men and women waited in rows to be seen and heard, were three private interview cubicles. Now he directed her towards one of these.

'If you'll just go in, Mrs Reid,' he said, holding the door open, 'I'll get your file and be with you straight away.'

He left her alone in a room with no windows and two plastic chairs on opposite sides of a heavy wooden desk. On the far wall, across from the door through which she had entered, was a second door, on which hung a sign prohibiting smoking and a notice advising visitors to obtain a receipt for all cash payments. Maureen sat down slowly. She remembered this room from a previous visit – the red stains on the carpet that she'd imagined were wine from tumblers knocked over during some office party with crêpe paper streamers and red serviettes, continuing on long after hours until only a few resolute couples remained behind to sway to the music and gather the trash. Again a thick wave of panic rocked her – by now a full hour must surely have passed since Albert had sent her for cigarettes. She was out of her seat and turning to leave when the far door opened and the young man came in.

'Sorry for the delay; we're all set now. As you can see from these sheets' – he sat down on the edge of the desk, opening a file and swinging it round so that neither one of them could see it clearly without craning – 'our records show that you were in receipt of full Housing Benefit less one fifth of rates or sixty-nine pence per week paid up until the second of the eighth ninety-two. However, our office notified the Housing Executive that you were no longer eligible for Income Support as of the twenty-first of the fifth ninety-two, though this information was not received by the NIHE for a further six weeks – '

He had stopped, it seemed, in mid-sentence, and now was gazing at Maureen with a curious intensity, as if she might have been able to contribute something vital to his own deliberations if only he could be sure they were thinking the same thing. With a decisive nod he stood up, leaving her file on the desk.

'Let me get Miss Burns in here with you. She was handling

your case until they gave it to me. Just wait here a minute, I'll fetch her, okay?'

He was gone before she could protest. She sat stiffly on the edge of the chair, her belongings clustered uncomfortably on her lap. Nerves made her unwrap the cigarettes and put the cellophane in her pocket before she remembered the No Smoking sign and the fact that Albert would notice when she gave him the box. Once again she rose to leave. A woman's voice, high-pitched and cheery, called her back.

'Hullo, Mrs Reid – Julie Burns. Please, have a seat. This shouldn't take long.'

Her voice was too strong for the confines of the room, but she had a pleasant appearance, her large, thick glasses and plump face creating an impression of good-natured efficiency. After a moment's shifting of hips and thighs she settled herself down in her seat and rested her elbows on the table's edge, her hands clasped beside a ball-point pen.

'Strictly speaking, Mrs Reid, this is a Housing Executive matter, but Miss Clarendon informed us that you had some question about why your husband's Income Support had been stopped as of the sixteenth of April, and since that termination resulted in a reduction in the total amount of Housing Benefit to which your husband is entitled, it seemed to them it might be best all around if you came and reviewed your case with us here.' The girl smiled brightly. 'Now. I think it'd be helpful if we go through these figures from the start of the year; that way I think you'll find that all our calculations are correct. You know, of course, that you and your husband are now considerably in arrears. Perhaps you could remind him that your failure to pay will jeopardise your eligibility for any future benefit from any governmental office, and that any further refusal to reimburse the appropriate departments could put you both potentially at risk.'

Again the girl smiled pleasantly. Maureen nodded, but there was nothing she could think to say.

'Shall we make a start, then?' the girl asked briskly. 'I've summarised the most recent developments in your case and itemised with the corresponding dates all the changes in your husband's income over the past six months, so if you'll just bear with me and save any questions you might have for the moment, I'll take you through the figures and ask you a few questions, and that should be us finished, okay?'

She asked her questions and Maureen responded, watching the girl's plump fingers travel over the coloured sheets in front of her. Her nails were clean and sculptured, her wrists surprisingly delicate for someone a little overweight. From the pocket of her skirt she produced a calculator and a small slip of paper, and Maureen followed the curves and lines of the figures as the girl added and subtracted them for her benefit. Her pen was an elegant instrument, thin and stylish like the ones that came boxed, together with a mechanical pencil and a fountain pen. Maureen imagined her receiving the set, a birthday or a Christmas gift from her boyfriend, imagined her smiling and her strong voice laughing with appreciation and delight.

'Well, that's it, Mrs Reid,' the girl said, replacing her pen. 'I hope that's answered any questions you might have had regarding your account. Please urge your husband to repay the advance; if you're unable to pay the full cash amount we can alway arrange to have a small percentage deducted each week from any benefit he's still entitled to receive. I'll make a note of your visit today in your file, but you should plan to come in to see us again soon.'

They rose together. As she left the building, Maureen glanced at the wall clock in the security hut, but the hands had stopped at twenty past twelve, over an hour before she'd left the house. The men in the hut were crowded around a small black-and-white monitor, and Maureen heard the mild voices of the sports commentator expressing his excitement in the aftermath of a goal. She hurried on.

The Road was still crowded, though the sky was threatening

rain. She hurried past the shops and manoeuvred the traffic, growing anxious each time the lights were against her. When she turned the corner into her own street she found it roped off, the yellow strips of plastic ribbon taut against the wind. There were land rovers and army vehicles at both ends of the street, and she could see soldiers, their weapons raised, crouching in the gardens behind the low, red-bricked walls. Bewildered, she followed a group of children down to the barriers where a policeman stood, legs apart, facing away from the street. Three of the boys ran up to him, their faces eager, jostling for space and speaking all at once.

'Here, mister, what's goin on?'

'What is it, mister? Is it a bomb?'

'Have they called in Felix, mister? Have they, mister, aye?'

The policeman ignored them. They continued to demand attention, reaching out, even, to tug at his sleeve, until a young UDR officer shouted to them to clear off.

Maureen stood awkwardly, uncertain how to proceed. At a shout from the direction of the rover, the officer by the barrier moved away, and Maureen watched him lean against the vehicle as someone inside handed him a flask. She glanced about her furtively, hardly daring to turn her head, then lifted the ribbon with two fingers and ducked underneath. A tall boy in khaki was standing in front of her when she straightened up.

'You can't go in there, miss,' the soldier said. A trio of constables standing by the rover with their hands inside their vests turned towards them, their visors so low over their eyes that they had to tilt their heads back in order to see.

'But that's my house there,' Maureen said, indicating the one with the front door missing. From the corner of her vision she saw the first constable returning. 'I've just been to the shop.'

The soldier shrugged. 'Sorry.'

Maureen stared back at him helplessly. He was very young, no more than sixteen, his face so soft and smooth she was certain he'd not yet started to shave. A plain, very slightly heavy boy, only his eyes were remarkable, cornflower blue and ever-steady, an infant's eyes before they begin to turn.

'Please,' she said, 'I have to get home.'

A second constable had joined the first and the two arrived together. They nodded curtly to the soldier who stepped aside to let them through.

'Problem?' the first one asked. His eyes were on Maureen but he had not directed his question to her. The soldier shook his head.

'Nah, I don't think so. This one says she lives here.'

'I do,' Maureen told them. 'I've only just come from the shop.'

The second constable nodded again, his eyes on the road behind her. 'Sorry, luv. No one's allowed in till the squad says it's safe.'

'But what is it?' she demanded petulantly. 'What's going on?'

'Nothing to worry about, luv, it's under control. Now, if you'll excuse us…'

Maureen scanned the length of the empty street. Mrs Mackie's washing spun slowly on the rotary line in her backyard, the breeze lifting the tiny frocks and blouses of her newborn. A child's tricycle stood upturned in mid-repair near the top of the street with one wheel missing, an oversized spanner and a box of screws abandoned beside it. Just below, a brown-and-yellow cat stalked gingerly along the low garden walls towards an overturned bin. Maureen hurried after the two policemen.

'But my husband,' she called, 'he wanted fags.'

'Well, I'm sure he'll wait for them,' the second constable said. 'Just you wait over there, there's a good lass. Stay well back, please, out of the way.'

'But he was asleep when I left him,' she continued, 'he didn't know I'd gone. He could still be in there.'

'No one's in those houses now, luv; everyone's been cleared out. Now you just wait away over there out of the road. As soon as it's safe we'll let you know.'

Maureen turned away, casting about for a place to sit down. He's not in the house, she thought. He could be anywhere, anywhere at all. A number of people had emerged from the houses just beyond the cordon to watch the activity, and for lack of an alternative, she headed their way. Apart from them and a few older residents who had not ventured beyond their front gates, the whole area was deserted. She felt the air growing damp and chill, and even as she approached, one or two people who'd been passing round cigarettes and speculating about the nature of the incident amongst themselves headed back indoors, glancing up at the sky. A pair of soldiers sprang up from their position behind a wall and ran a few paces towards the top of the street. Maureen turned to watch them, her mind on the last time Albert had disappeared. She'd gone round to a friend's house to pass the time. The woman had had her front room redecorated, had offered Maureen her old carpet and suite; they'd just poured the tea when Albert arrived. He'd raised his fist though he had not hit her, then he'd hauled her off across three streets back to their own house.

Someone shouted from the top end of the street and Maureen flinched; a policeman appeared walking swiftly, both hands on his gun. Her eyes were drawn towards a child sitting on the kerb opposite the yellow ribbon, wearing an adult's court shoes and absorbed in the effort of removing her cardigan. Maureen carried her belongings over and squatted down. The child glanced up with a look of distracted concentration and silently presented the buttons to Maureen for help. She set the milk and the cheese and the other purchases down and took the toddler on her knee, tugging gently at the knitted garment, her eyes watchful for her husband's approach.

Undertow

I T WAS CLOSE to September and the date of the wedding when my father started bringing us to Castlerock. After breakfast we'd board the first train from Central Station that went south to Lambeg and Lisburn before turning north and arriving eventually beside the sea. We'd spend the rest of the day there on the rocks above the beach, hurling stones into the oncoming waves and fishing without bait until it was time to catch the last train from Derry home. The train leaned hard into the left shoulder just before the platform came into sight, and as we moved towards the exits to be ready when it stopped, I would watch the reflection of the streetlights on the far side of the Lagan wink on the spiral whenever a fish rose up for air.

What's that flashing? I'd asked my father the first time I'd seen it.

Fairy lights, he answered.

Bullshit, Ricky said, under his breath. He was five years my senior, thirteen and no longer a baby; rebellion came easily to him like a dog. We were fifty yards from the platform and the sign above him told him No, but still he'd thrown his weight against the window, pulled it down and thrust his head out into the wind. He would not take my father's hand as we stepped down from the train.

My mother was sitting at the kitchen table with John-O Noonan when we got home. John-O's fingers were yellow from nail-tip to knuckle and his whole hand twitched with desire; there was no smoking allowed in my mother's house.

It's happened again, she told my father.

Has it indeed? What's it of this time?

I'm flat out of paint, she said, so you'll have to go get some. I won't have that damn thing on the side of my house.

After our tea we went out to look at it. This time they'd painted flags and emblems, and every letter of the words that went with them was outlined in black and at least two feet high. The last time they'd done a map of the country with a pair of armed soldiers on either side, and before that there'd been a bright yellow shield on a powder blue background, and a list of the names of the most recent dead. Each time my mother had covered it over by climbing a stepladder and chucking buckets of paint at the house.

When do they do it, that's what I'd like to know, John-O said. He lived in the house which terraced ours, where he spent his days minding his sister's children and keeping his eye on the Help Wanted columns, in case something came up that my father could do. He shook his head with slow admiration. How the hell do they do it when youse're here all the time?

I wish to God I could catch them at it, my mother said. I don't care who they are. That's the last bit of painting they'd ever do.

It's a real shame, my father said.

Don't start with me, Joe, my mother told him. I've no time for hoods. I'll get that paint myself if I have to.

First thing tomorrow, he answered. The shops'll be closed now, anyway.

The next day my father and I lay on till eleven. My mother was working at the kitchen table when I went downstairs to make us tea. She'd been working steadily since early that morning but the sound of machinery hadn't disturbed us, because each sequin and pearl was sewn on by hand. By this time the shell of the dress was nearly finished – the bodice and skirt, the two mutton sleeves, the veil, the headdress, and the wide, four-foot train. She had still to complete the undergarments, and she'd promised to hem the girl's linens, embroider their edges, and inscribe the corners with the first letter of her name.

Your brother's gone out, my mother told me, so it's up to you to look after your father. Don't let him come home without that paint. I stood just behind her while the kettle boiled, skewering beads on her upright needle as soon as she'd fastened the previous one. Oh here, listen, she said, and reached under the fabric in search of her purse. The table was lost under cover of satin, a full bolt of chiffon lay unwrapped on the floor, and thick books of patterns sat on each chair, their insides fat with slips of paper, receipts, and newsprint torn into strips to mark a page. A spool of white thread, luv, she said, giving me money, say you want the kind for all types of fabric, and get me at least two hundred yards. I'd ask your daddy but you know he won't do it.

Because I don't think it's right, my father said from the threshold. Taking advantage of a foolish woman when you know rightly there won't be a wedding on the twenty-first. You can't have a wedding without a groom.

More's the pity, my mother said, and unnecessarily switched on her machine.

Well I won't be part of it, my father continued. I will not add to that girl's disappointment.

For God's sake, Joe, my mother said, it's none of my business what they want the clothes for. That girl placed an order same as anyone else.

A wedding gown's different, my father told her. Especially this.

I didn't ask to hear her life's story, Joe, my mother told him, and what she does with her money is her own affair. If she wants to waste it on fortune-tellers that's got nothing to do with me.

I think we are obligated to protect the innocent, my father said quietly.

Fair enough, my mother answered, but only if they're mine. That girl pays good money, in advance and on time. I've got this family to worry about, Joe.

We spoke no more about it, though my father refused to come

in the shop with me when I went in to purchase thread. We bought two tins of paint, a tray, and a roller, and were in the sitting room stirring the tins when Ricky came home with a sackful of chestnuts.

How come they're called conkers? I asked my father.

Why d'you think? Ricky said. He took one whose green armoured shell had not yet broken and slapped it, palm open, against his head.

It began with a farmer, my father answered, who owned a good bit of land not far from Mullan Head. He was a man who didn't like to spend money, and it's not like he didn't have it to spend. Every night he sat in the dark so he wouldn't have to run the electric, and all the beasts on his farm had bad teeth and were spindly because he was too cheap to give them a decent feed. Now there was a tree on that land and the farmer didn't like it. Its shade kept him cold, he said, and it made his house dark. He blamed the tree for his own mean nature, and one day he decided, I'll cut the thing down. But the tree saw him coming with his rolled-up sleeves and his heavy boots and the toothy new saw in his hand. It got so frightened it shook and heaved, and a whole shower of chestnuts fell on the farmer, sticking and pricking him with their rubbery spines. He was so bruised and battered he spent six weeks in hospital, and as soon as he got out he picked up and left. Then a husband and wife with two little children, a boy and a wee girl about your age, came to live in the house. They put a swing on the tree and built a conservatory, and the house is so full of light now that they built a train past it, and if you're a good wee girly this evening and eat all your peas, I'll show you it tomorrow on the way to Castlerock.

Joe, my mother said from the other room. How old is your daughter?

So why don't all trees throw conkers all the time?

Cuz it's all bollocks, that's why, Ricky said. They fall cuz the stems rot, that's why its easy to knock em down.

You know what your problem is, Ricky? my mother called to him.

Humankind has grown impatient, my father answered. The cold facts of science take less time to tell.

The side of our house stayed white for six days. On the morning of the seventh my mother noticed the additional shadow when she stepped outside to bring in the milk.

Joe, she called from the bottom of the stairs, c'mere till you see this.

From the room next to mine I heard my parents' bed creak as my father rolled onto his back and sighed.

Ah, Belle, he said, it's not even seven.

They've left a ladder, my mother said, and I'll tell you right now they're not getting it back.

Not very good, is it? John-O said an hour or so later. Still in his dressing gown and pyjamas, he'd seen our door lying open when he'd let the cat out and had jumped the low fence that ran between us, calling our names as he hurried into the house. My mother, lugging a tarpaulin and paint thinner, had nearly run over him as she backed out the door.

Different artist, my father answered. This wee fella's got no sense of colour.

It's God awful, John-O said. I'm with you, missus – get rid of it. That bloody thing's hard on the eyes.

It's going today, my mother said firmly. I've a girl coming by for a fitting tomorrow, and this will not be the first thing she sees.

What time tomorrow? my father said suddenly.

For a moment my mother looked like she'd bitten her tongue. I know what you're thinking, Joe, she said, and it's not going to happen.

Go on, Belle. What time's she coming?

I should have known you'd pull something like this, my mother said bitterly. Why can't you stay out of it? It's got nothing to do with you.

Right! John-O said. See youse all later.

I just want to talk to her, Belle, that's all.

What for? What good'll it do? She's not getting a refund, you know, even if you do manage to make her change her mind.

C'mon now, folks, John-O said, don't do this outside.

It's not just about money, my father answered. It's her state of mind. What's going to happen to her two weeks from Friday? I'm not convinced she's going to survive.

Alright, Joe, my mother said. I give up. Stay in if you want to tomorrow; just get the hell out of my way today.

There now, John-O said cheerfully, that's better. Youse two had me worried there for a while.

We'd missed the first train to Derry, but we did catch the second. Ricky stayed behind to help my mother; intending to keep the ladder as evidence, she'd said no when he'd asked for it and offered to let him paint the wall instead. When we arrived in Castlerock we headed at once for our regular cafe, where we each ordered a fish and chip dinner and my father explained why fish had it so bad – because they bore grudges, resenting all those who'd stood on four feet at the birth of Jesus, and the dove for finding the olive branch, and all the rest of the animal kingdom for having a place set aside for them on the ark. It didn't matter that God had conferred on them wisdom, that He'd warned them about the flood in advance. And so they are regularly captured and eaten, they fall ill easily and are tormented by cats, and though they gasp with the effort of trying to buy freedom with the secrets the Almighty had shared, they can never produce the human words necessary, never can make themselves understood. And that, said my father, is apt punishment for arrogance – that they die ignominiously, out of their element, impressive only because of their size.

Then our dinners were ready and he went up to fetch them. He came back with two plates and a plastic lemon, which he set down on the table next to the salt. If Ricky'd been with us he'd have been embarrassed, and my father would have explained yet again how he met my mother. She'd been the new girl at the local chippy where he went occasionally for a take-away, and he'd asked her for a wedge of lemon, which naturally enough the shop didn't have. The dinner rush was at its most frantic when my mother put on her coat and took her umbrella and went down to a grocer two blocks away to buy my father a bagful of lemons with her own money, because there was something about his face she fancied. At this establishment, my father said as if I'd protested, my custom is valued. Did she really empty them out on top of you? I asked him. Right in my lap, he said. There must have been two or three dozen at least.

And then what happened?

Then? Then your mother was sacked and I was ejected. We never went near the place again.

After our dinner we walked to the beach. A buttress of rocks spilled into the sea, their surfaces pitted with shallow depressions, warm water puddles of algae and snails and keyhole limpets whose airtight seals resisted all efforts to pry their shells loose. A man hurled a stick and his dog sailed after and caught it each time in its open jaws, the wide arc of its body in motion continuing on into the water with the same compact force of those who ran barefoot from one rock to another to fling themselves off the final one, their knees to their chests and their arms wrapped around them, their hair and clothes still heavy with water from the previous jump. There's our friend, said my father, and I turned to see a horse approaching, its rider bouncing like a ball on a string as the horse's hooves pummelled the surf, leaving prints that the tide made more cavernous, brown sugar sand tumbling in on all sides. They'd been there every day since we first started coming. The man lived by himself in a one-room caravan staked to flat ground just beyond Castlerock, and he kept his horse on a small slab of pasture which belonged to no one and which he'd cleared himself. He's a nutter, Ricky had said when my father told us. Everyone says so. You must learn the difference between fraud and fiction, Ricky, my father said. It's true, Ricky'd said sullenly. There's even a petition to get him put out. The darkness of Mankind is truly untellable, my father said later, more to himself than to either of us. It shouldn't surprise me but it always does.

The man rode bareback and the horse wore no bridle, yet they pulled up beside us with the flourish expected when reins are drawn tight, hot breath expelled from the horse's nostrils, sand splashing over us with each sweep of its tail.

You're late today, the man said.

I know it, my father said. What about ye?

The man shrugged. Yerself?

We're alright, aren't we, luv? said my father. Do you still want a ride?

C'mon up, luv, the man said, and I reached for his hand. Up close the horse smelled like brass and worn leather; I filled my fists with its oily mane, my father put his hand on my ankle and I felt the knees of the man behind me press against the horse's ribs. We walked past the mouth of the tunnel, that long stretch of darkness from which trains hurtle out, startling their passengers with the sudden proximity of sand and seawater, of gulls suspended above black shards of rock. Then we turned and came back at a canter, my father too on the animal's strong back, past boys Ricky's age who were playing football, past new groups of people sitting on jackets drinking beer and soft drinks from oversized tins, up the very steps which led to the street. Look after yourself now, my father said. You worry too much, the other man told him, and urged the horse through the small crowd of children that had gathered around him and headed back the way we'd just come.

In Coleraine while we waited to transfer I stood at the edge of the platform to watch the incoming train, signalled by sirens and the lowering of booms, a mad dash of assorted pedestrians and small dogs on leads hurrying from one side of the road to the other before the train, with the same graceful movements of things buoyed by water, came round the corner and eased into the station.

Stand back now, my father said. Let them get off. But my eyes were not on the entrance but on the red diamond in the centre of the train's yellow face. We'd chosen a car that was practically empty, so once we were settled with our tickets ready, our crisps on the table, our feet outstretched towards the seat across from us, and our coats and umbrellas on the rack above our heads, I asked my father to tell me the story he'd promised the last time.

Oh yes, he said, I'd nearly forgotten. When the iron horse was first brought to Ireland, the other animals found it a bad-mannered beast. It was loud and filthy and single-minded, it stopped on no whim or for any diversion, just proceeded directly from A to B. To be so oblivious to the world around you was a dangerous condition, the other beasts said, for what if one of them happened to stop in its path? But once they realised that the train only ran on the tracks set down for it, and only at more or less predictable times, they began to enjoy its daily passage. They even grew rather possessive, and boasted about it when they'd had too much to drink. Our train can beat any bird flying, the beasts would say loudly, whenever birds were around to hear – which naturally the birds took as a challenge, and eventually they sent someone over to accept. But the two parties couldn't agree on the details of the contest, until finally the bird representative said How about this: you set the distance, and we'll set the course. The beasts were confident their man could travel over any terrain, so they said Okay, but we're not crossing water – and then congratulated themselves for being so clever. About the same time as all this was happening a new model of train was intro-duced. This one was even faster, the beasts read in the advertise-ments they found in the newspapers that passengers tossed from the windows, along with their cigarette butts and their empty tins. When the birds found this out they flew into a panic, but agreed to play one hand of pontoon, the winner to decide which train would be run. Three times the dealer peeled cards from the deck; then the birds (with a hand adding up to fifteen) and the beasts (with a five, a two, and the queen of spades) decided to ask for just one more. Twenty! the birds said when they got theirs, and if they'd been playing poker they'd have been hard to beat, for what they had in front of them was a straight flush of hearts. The beasts sucked their teeth and said they were sorry but they didn't mean it, for their hidden card was the three of diamonds, and with the ace they'd been given they'd just made twenty-one.

Listen! my father said as our train passed another, and I heard in the jolt and clatter of the tracks the sound of a deck of iron cards being shuffled. What about the race? I asked. Did the train beat the birds? Well, no, my father said. Sure the beasts had forgotten that a train can't run if there aren't any tracks. The birds chose a course that never crossed water, but it also didn't pass through A or B. As soon as they discovered the situation, all the earth-moving beasts got stuck in right away, but no one could lift the rails from the stack in the depot, let alone move them to the ground they'd prepared. It was very frustrating, my father conceded, his arm growing heavy around my shoulders and his own gaze wandering to the scenery outside. I watched the outgoing tracks sprinting beside us, and imagined a pair of simultaneous tunnels, blind, flowered snouts and efficient fingers churning the soil up from below.

We reached our gate just as John-O was leaving, and it was clear from my mother's expression that she'd been trying to ease him out for some time. When John-O saw us his face brightened. My mother's brows drew together like curtains; she exhaled audibly and went back inside.

Talk sense to this woman, John-O pleaded, walking backwards in front of my father. She won't listen to me.

The dress was loosely assembled now. My father stooped to gather a fallen crinoline and struggled to drape it over the back of a chair, the garment appearing to defy gravity until my mother took it off him and dropped it back onto the floor.

I want to go to the council, get a sign put up.

A sign to say what?

Keep Off, that's what, my mother said irritably. I'm tired of wasting my time and money. It should be the council's problem, not mine.

Don't let her do it, John-O said to my father. She'll only annoy them. You're lucky they've let you paint the thing over. How many times has it been now? Three?

Four. If the council won't listen I'll go to the police.

You don't know who they are, John-O said. They could put you out first.

Is that right? Well just let them try.

It's not worth it, John-O said earnestly, even if it is just kids. Kids can be wee bastards, too, you know.

Where's Ricky? my father said after John-O went home.

Upstairs with Jason. Can't you hear that damn racket?

Go tell him to lower it, luv, my father said, and I had to twice before Ricky would. When I came down the second time my father, whose hands were cool even in summer, had placed his palms on the back of her neck, right where the spine makes its small mountain ridge, and was kneading her shoulders in generous handfuls, his own cheek resting on the top of her head.

I'm still going to do it, Joe, she said.

Ricky's friend left a short while later, and my father herded me upstairs to bed. I'm not tired, I told him, I slept on the train. Go on, luv, he said, lie down, close your eyes. Don't you worry. Everything's going to be okay. Here – tell me three things you saw today and I'll make you a story.

A tub in a field, I said. And a tree island. And a whole fence full of plastic bags.

Right, he said, here goes the first one. There once was a king whose greatest wish was for peace and quiet. Though his country had not been to war for many years, and though the land was fertile and the climate kind, still his people fought and bickered amongst themselves, and the king, as the arbiter of all disputes, found himself again and again called away from love or meditation to pass judgement on a trivial disagreement, or soothe the ego of some individual who felt insulted or slighted by somebody else. The king consulted with the greatest minds in study and politics, but no one could offer any good advice. Finally the king commissioned a wizard who said he'd cast a spell that'd do the trick – he'd send a fog so thick it'd cover the land like heavy cream, and when it cleared all those thinking evil thoughts about another would be revealed for what they were. The king agreed, and for nine days afterwards a fog was on them, thicker on the ninth day than it had been on the first. On the tenth day the sun was so brilliant that most folks just marvelled – until they heard the embarrassed cries of the evil thinkers, caught stark naked in their bathtubs out in their fields for all the world to see. For the wizard had set an additional spell, so that all the vicious and petty people would be taking a bath at just the same time. The tubs that exposed them have been there ever since, collecting rain for the livestock to drink. The land itself has changed hands so often, hardly a soul remembers why they're there now. Are you asleep yet?

Not yet, I said, but I already was.

Not so long ago the Hardest Working Couple in the World was living with their children in Island Magee. Though the mother and father had earned the title by working continuously for more than ten months, even so they barely had enough for the bills and the shopping, and though Christmas was coming they hadn't been able to buy any gifts. On Christmas Eve on the road home from work the woman met an old man with such heavy wrinkles he had to use a forked branch to keep his brows up. What can I do to please my children? the woman asked him, because she was desperate for someone to talk to. We've laboured long and hard, but we're no richer for it. We don't even have stockings to hang over the hearth. Take one empty sack for each in your family and tie them to the fence that keeps your cows in, the old man said, and tomorrow your children will thank you for it. The woman did what he'd told her, and the next morning every sack was full of chocolate and oranges, picture books and pens and mechanical toys. A month or so later it was one child's birthday, and again his parents had no money to spare. On the off chance of a second miracle the woman tied another sack to the fence – and sure enough the next morning it was so heavy it pulled the fence after it on its way to the ground. Why should we work, the woman wondered as she watched her son enjoying his presents, when all we want can be had for the asking? But the spirit that filled the bags was no eejit; it knew what their game was when later that night the woman and her husband covered their fence with empty bags. The next morning all the sacks looked full from a distance, but up close it was clear they held only wind. The worst of it is the mother and father never learned their lesson: they kept leaving sacks on the fence for generations, and wasted so much time waiting for nothing they lost their title of Hard Working Couple to a rival team from Markethill. And that's why there's plastic bags on the fences, because people are greedy past the point of good sense.

My mother put down her scissors and looked at me. He told you this.

I nodded.

What do you think of your father's stories?

I think he should sell them, John-O said. A letter requesting my father's attendance at an interview that afternoon had arrived the same morning, and John-O, who had spotted the post in the Job Finder listings, was waiting in our kitchen to see him off. He'd make a fortune, John-O continued. Youse could get out of Belfast, buy a big house with at least fifteen bedrooms, a huge garden and a two-car garage – you could buy a good car with that kind of money. That's what I'd do if I was him.

Well, said my mother, he left a part out of this one. Farmers put bags on their fences to frighten their cows, luv. It's to keep them away from the wire so they don't try to get into other people's fields.

You could even go somewhere exotic, John-O said. I hear the weather's brilliant in Florida. An annual rainfall of less than three inches and sunshine ten months out of every year.

Alright? said my father on his way past the kitchen. He'd come down the stairs at a run, his hand already reaching for the outside door.

Where's your tie? my mother demanded.

He patted his pocket. It's too warm, Belle. I'll put it on when I get there.

No, said my mother. Come over here. Stop fussing, Joe, she continued preemptively, it won't take a minute. Standing behind him she tugged at his waistband, and the cuffs of his trousers snapped to attention. How's that? Too tight?

I could borrow a belt, my father suggested.

It's done now, my mother said, and ran her razor down the short seam at the back of the garment and plucked the torn stitches out with a pin. Hand me that thread, luv, she said, and I snapped off a strand and moistened its end, and she pushed it through the eye of the needle she held with the same hand that gripped the thin fabric of my father's summer suit. There, she said after a minute, tugging his sleeves and smoothing his shoulders, her fingers running over his lapels till he caught her wrists and drew her to him, placing a kiss on each open palm. Go on, get out of here, she said, you'll be late, but she stood at our gate with me and John-O and even waved back to him as he waited for the bus.

Alright, everybody, she said as the bus pulled away, show's over, back to work. But the expected client was late for her fitting, and when John-O sent his niece over with cream buns later, my mother agreed she had made enough progress to stop and have

144

one with a quick cup of tea. It was some time after that when the girl rang our bell.

C'mon in, my mother shouted from the kitchen where she'd taken a break from replacing a zipper to clean the grit out of Ricky's wounds. He'd been fighting again, though he wouldn't admit it. He'd told my mother he'd slipped on the ladder she'd told him expressly to stay away from, knowing the clout she was likely to give him would have been worse if he'd told her the truth. That's it there, my mother said before the girl could apologise, go ahead and try it on.

The girl took a step towards the dress and looked around her, at the no longer sterile roll of cotton and the bottle of alcohol on the kitchen counter, at Ricky's arm in my mother's firm grasp, at the teetering piles of new jeans and chinos purchased on sale from shops in the town, every one of them too long in the legs to be worn immediately and belonging to boys from our estate.

Where d'you want me?

Right here, my mother said. Ricky, go do something. He gave me a look as she released him, corked the bottle, and tossed the used swabs, but he needn't have bothered. I remembered the last time he'd gotten in trouble. He'd been one of a crowd of children who'd demolished a car that had been in an accident and was moved temporarily to the side of the road. The front left-hand corner had been shorn off on impact, but apart from that there'd been little damage, and those who'd come running when they heard the collision were saying it was too bad the driver was uninsured when a boy took a stick and smashed the taillights. Within half an hour all the windows were broken, the roof had caved in, and someone had started an ineffectual fire in the foam rubber stuffing they'd pulled out of the backseat. That afternoon Ricky and I went out with my father, who'd been in town when it happened, and found the owner of the car sitting on the kerb. Whose fault was it? my father asked him. It was his, the man said, but what does it matter? He's already got witnesses to say it was me. Later that night I'd informed on my brother, but my father said only, Yes, I know, and told me a story about Belfast Courthouse. A long time ago its four walls were formed out of living flora, a garden attended by Justice herself. But the crimes of Mankind had been so dazzling they had left Justice blind, and with no one to tend it the building itself had turned into stone, the grey marble leaves and flowers blackened by soot and ringing the pillars outside the court the only reminder of what Justice once was. So is Ricky not going to get beaten, then? I'd asked. No, he said, that's not the point. People don't often get what's coming to them, one way or the other. The important thing is to keep trying to make sure they do.

The dress opened and closed by button only. At least three dozen ran from the small of the back towards the high collar, each one fastened through a tight elastic loop. My mother lay a board across two tins of paint and tested it briefly; then the girl stepped onto it, the heavy folds of her skirts gathered high in both hands.

Are you redecorating? she asked.

All the time, my mother said. Lift up now; that's right.

I need to buy wallpaper myself, the girl said, holding her arms away from her sides. I was trying to get the house ready for Friday, but it's taking forever. I still have another two bedrooms to go, and I've done nothing else but that house all week.

How many bedrooms, altogether?

Five – well, four and a half, really. There's a wee room at the top that'd suit a child. It used to be part of the other back bedroom, but I put up a partition. We can always take it down again if we need the space. She dropped her arms on my mother's instruction and smiled. I retiled the bathroom, too, and lay new lino in the kitchen. I bought seeds to replant the garden, and a trellis for the side of the house, but I won't have the chance till after we've moved in.

If you don't mind me asking, my mother said, where are you getting the money for all this?

I won the pools, the girl said simply. I played the numbers Fortuna gave me, and I won about two thousand pounds. My mother was on her knees adjusting the hem so the lace trim of the underskirt would show more clearly; she glanced up at the girl but did not pause. She's been right about other things, too, the girl continued. She knew my sister miscarried the first time, and told her she was pregnant again before she knew herself. She can tell things about you just by holding your hand.

I don't think I'd like that, my mother said. Turn this way, please.

I know, the girl said, I thought I wouldn't, either. But it's okay, it's nothing like I expected. She's awful good. My girlfriend saved for two years to put a deposit on a trip to Corfu, and the first thing Fortuna says to her is You're going to travel. And she told my mum she was going to get better and it was six months before she took sick again.

I don't know, my mother said. Here, try the veil on. The pools thing's impressive, but the rest of it sounds pretty familiar.

You should go, the girl said generously. She knew wee things about me I never told anyone. I was ill myself last year and she knew about it. She even knew what was in my head at the time.

Upstairs Ricky kicked a football through the door of his room onto the landing and down the stairs into the hall. I saw the ball bounce on its way past the kitchen and then heard the sound of it striking wood. Go easy! my mother warned him when he came in, but he only grinned.

Da's back, he said.

My father seemed surprised when he saw us together, the girl on her platform, my mother on her knees, myself on a chair in charge of the pincushion, and Ricky with the football under his arm, spoiling his supper with the last cream bun.

This is my husband, my mother said through her teeth. The girl nodded quickly, flushed and self-conscious, but at that height even her awkwardness was elevated to grace. She wore the veil as it's worn after vows, the thin film of gauze spilling over her shoulders like freshly brushed hair. My father stood beneath her, gazing up.

You look very beautiful, he said.

It's lovely, isn't it? the girl said eagerly.

It's alright, my mother said, but I knew she was pleased. I'd helped her select the low, smooth bodice, and approved the change to sleeves which began off the shoulder and tapered to a point just past the wrist. I'd been there when she'd added a bustle, and replaced a full skirt which just brushed the ground with one more narrow, with a heavy train. Think elegant, my mother had said as we looked through the patterns. What we don't want is to make the thing vulgar. Feminine, yes, but not delicate, necessarily. Handsome? I'd offered. That's it, she'd said. Whatever else happens, at least she'll look strong.

We won't be much longer, my mother told him. Why don't you go next door for awhile? I'll send Ricky over when the supper's ready.

No need, my father said heartily, almost before John-O came into the room. John-O, this is the wee girl that's getting married.

Oh, aye? John-O said. Congratulations. What's your fiancée do, by the way?

Not now, my mother said sharply. We're not finished here.

Fortuna says he'll be a baker. She says he'll come home with flour in his pockets, and he'll leave white footprints on the carpet when he takes off his shoes. She says I'll never smell another woman on him, only bread from the oven and marzipan.

My father's mouth opened, but when no words were coming John-O stopped waiting and turned back to the girl.

Is he from round here, your boyfriend?

Oh no, she said, he's from the country. That's why I got a house near Bellevue. Fortuna said he'd like it, being close to Cave Hill.

An outdoorsy type, is he?

He'll like having a garden, the girl said, he can make anything grow. I was just going to get roses, put a few bushes at the front of

the house, but Fortuna said I should invest in a fruit tree or something, since she didn't see us moving house for a while. Course,
I'm useless with flowers, and I can't cook. That's why Fortuna
thinks we'll make a good match.

Right, my mother said, that's us finished. Could youse all get
out while she changes, please?

After they'd gone she brought out the linens, four sets of sheets
and eight pillowcases so heavy that when she set them down on
the kitchen table loose scraps of thread and less durable fabrics
jumped up in protest, and the hair around all three of our faces
was moved by the puff of air she'd displaced. Your shift and
things aren't finished yet, she told the girl, but I'll have them all
ready for Wednesday. You can come and collect them any time
after noon.

Can't I have them delivered? It's just I still have so much to do.

If you want, my mother said. It's a bit risky. Personally I like to
have a good look at a thing before I pay the bill. But it's up to you.
If you want them sent over I need the balance off you now.

That's okay, the girl said, I brought money with me. The bills
she counted onto the table were still crisp and in sequence like
the sheaves that spill from unmarked envelopes or are stacked and
banded in open briefcases and pushed across deserted ware-
house floors, and I thought of a trick that John-O had taught me,
a way to fold bank notes to make the face printed on them smile
or frown. That only works with the real ones, my father had
added. All the forged ones do is grin.

It really is lovely, the girl said as she pulled on her coat.

I think it suits you, my mother said, following her out. You'll
look well on the day. Are you getting your hair done?

Aye, I am, I'm putting it up. I brought in that picture you gave
me, the one you drew the first time I came here. The girl in the
salon said she could do something that'd set off the dress. I hope
it's okay – I nearly rang you up to get your opinion, but you'd have
to have seen it, really, to know. Here, why don't you come? she

suggested suddenly. I've booked a wee room for the reception after – there's one right beside where they do the service.

Sorry, my mother said, but I'm up to my eyes in work at the minute. Thanks all the same.

It'd only be for an hour. There's another couple booked in for one o'clock. Please come. And think about going to see Fortuna. It's only five pounds for a palm reading, ten if you want the crystal ball.

My father sighed as he closed the door after her. So what d'you think? John-O asked him. Is she crazy?

No more than most.

Will there not be a wedding, then? I asked.

You never know, luv, he said. She might find someone yet. It's easier now, certainly, than it used to be. A long time ago there were rules about who you could marry. If a man fell in love with a widow, for example, he couldn't marry her unless he was a widower himself.

That's true enough, John-O said before my mother could protest. I heard about that on Celebrity Squares.

One boy in particular, my father continued, fell in love with a girl who was already married. Many years went by and the young man grew old, but he stayed a bachelor, for he knew he'd be no good as a husband without her as his wife. He spent his time writing bad poetry and romantic letters which of course he never sent, for the woman herself was happily married, and whatever his feelings he'd never do anything that might cause her pain. He wished no harm on her husband, either. In fact, he was almost resigned to a life as Love's martyr when word reached him that his beloved had been widowed at last. After a period of respectful courtship he crossed his fingers and made his proposal; naturally he was over the moon when she said yes. To get round the rules he married a tree the following morning, chopped it down to be widowed around three o'clock, and that very evening joined his sweetheart in holy matrimony.

Married a tree, my mother repeated.

You see? Ricky said. If that girl's not crazy, what d'you call him?

It's all true, John-O protested. I remember the programme.

If there is a wedding, I asked my mother, are you going to go?

I am not, she said. She glanced at my father. And neither are you.

Maybe we ought to, he said. She shouldn't be alone.

She's got family. Her sister'll be there. She'll be alright.

Aye, she will, Ricky said. If she can't find a man she can marry a tree.

What's going to happen? I asked my father when he came in later to kiss me good-night. I don't know, luv, he said. Maybe she'll be lucky. Lots of people are.

I rolled towards the weight of him on the edge of my bed, and for a long time his fingers brushed the hair from my brow and temple, smoothing and shaping it over my ear. We did not speak. I kept my eyes closed when he finished, and he stood up without asking if I were asleep. I opened them only when his back was turned and saw my mother in the doorway, watching him come.

Well? she asked. How'd it go?

He took her hand from her pocket and turned it over.

You'll have a long life, he said, and two lovely children. But you'll live in a house that brings only trouble, and you'll marry a man who'll be good for nothing and make your life seem longer still.

Did it not go well, then.

Not very.

Why, what happened?

He tilted her palm for a further reading but she put her other hand on his shoulder, and he stopped and frowned and looked at her arm.

Tell me, she said.

What's there to tell? I'm thirty-eight years old; I've not worked in six years. How good could it go?

But you got an interview.

Yes, he said. There is that.

There'll be other jobs, she said, and though I could not see her face with the hall light behind her I imagined the way it had summoned its power the first morning she'd discovered they'd painted our wall.

We went to Portrush on the day of the wedding. My father asked John-O to come along with us, but he'd promised to take his nephew and niece to the zoo. There was a polar bear there that they wanted to see, which took two steps backwards for every twelve it walked front, and an elephant seal that spent most of its time under the water and only pretended to enjoy human company. Why does he do that? I'd asked my father. We'd been lucky; we were far from the plexiglas when we saw the beast spew, the small group who'd gathered to laugh or admire stumbling backwards in confusion, holding their soaked shirts and blouses away from their skin. He's proud, my father explained, and he values his privacy. This is his way of pointing back.

It was strange not to transfer when we got to Coleraine. On good days the cast-iron bridge that vaulted the tracks was warm to the touch as I held onto the rail, the pigeons so bold on the ledge just beneath us that they barely noticed when we passed, their heads subsiding between their shoulders, the dreary stains and splotches of their city colours made as beautiful in the sunlight as the faint iridescence around their necks. But this time we stayed seated and watched other passengers collect their belongings and empty out of the small wooden doors which let the breeze in. A few people came on but walked through to Smoking, then the doors were snapped shut along the length of the carriage, I heard someone whistle, and the train pulled away.

The forecast had been hopeful, so we'd brought food for a picnic. In a concrete shelter which faced the sea my mother announced the contents of the sandwiches she'd made and distributed them to us with a packet of crisps and carton of orange, and for a while there was only the sound of crunch and swallow, and the spluttering sighs of liquid reversing through straws.

A gull stalked the wall that bordered the walkway, harassing a dog in the shade underneath. We threw scraps and the gull descended, riding the air with wings outstretched as if it were lowered by invisible strings, and soon more arrived, each one as possessive of the air space in front of us as if it had the right of being there first. In the interest of fairness I threw a crust to the dog. It raised its chin to watch the bread land but apart from that it didn't move. No, my father agreed when I showed him, they aren't very intelligent. The Sixth Day of Creation was a busy one for God; the dogs had to wait for several hours while He was fashioning the other beasts, and by that time all the best attributes had been given out. Loyalty and patience and an affectionate nature seemed more attractive to them than intelligence at the time. Not such a poor choice, my mother said. No, my father responded. I don't think they regret it.

Here, Da, Ricky said, wait'll you see. He called the dog by some generic name, and the animal rose from its haunches and came over, smiling and nodding and wagging its tail.

Sit, Ricky said, and the dog sat down indifferently like a man whose thoughts are somewhere else. Give us your paw, he said, and the animal did so with bored amusement, as if it were humouring a tiresome friend. Hand me a hammer, Ricky said with the same inflection, and the dog withdrew its right arm and lifted its left. See? Ricky said. You can tell'm anything. It's all got to do with your tone of voice. What do you want me to make him do?

Have him roll over, my mother said.

Fly round, Ricky said, addressing the dog, go on, fly round. The dog stretched lazily, its rump raised and waving till its chest touched the ground. That's it; now – throw bowlers! Ricky commanded, but the dog looked at him sceptically, its eyebrows raised. Throw bowlers, he said again, like an invitation, and the dog lay its ear on the tarmac and rolled onto its back. For some time preoccupied with its own hips and shoulders, it finally rose and shook itself violently, spattering us with flecks of saliva, fragments of glass, sand, and lawn clippings and other footpath garbage. When it had finished it calmly accepted the crisps Ricky fed it and offered its ears to my father's caress.

The dog followed briefly when we headed for Waterworld, but soon was distracted by the sight of something at the far end of the beach. Let him go, son, my mother said when Ricky called after him, then slipped her arm through his as if she found walking difficult and she needed his help. They don't allow dogs where we're going, anyway.

The complex featured a selection of swimming pools and three water slides, twisting tunnels of bright coloured plastic which plunged thirty feet into the water, jiggling like innards each time they were used, and a hidden machine which produced six-foot waves. The smell of chlorine was sharp close to the pools, and even the foyer was warm and damp. In the changing rooms at the back of the building wet swimsuits and towels slapped to the ground beside the benches and outside the stalls with the finality of things attracted by magnets, and steam rose from the threshold of water through which all new arrivals were required to pass. For a while I just stood by the railing and watched others pop from the slides with all the surprise of people whose chairs have been pulled out from under them. A siren erupted every half hour, and those on the lip of the pool with their feet in the water twisted round on their palms and slipped over the side. Then the machine was switched on and the contents of the pool sloshed over its edges, slapping the steps at the opposite end where the concrete floor hurried up at an anxious angle, and the water was so shallow it was still almost white. Because Ricky dared me I climbed the scaffolding which led to the slides. Someone behind me gave me a push, and I was carried down on a thin sheet of water, my hips riding furiously up the sides of the tube. All I could see was the white mouth of the exit swinging far in front, at the centre of a world which was otherwise yellow, backlit and uniform and almost translucent, and I thought of small, pallid insects and what they might see traversing the contours of delicate blossoms, following the easy confluence of grooves.

When we got home my mother of course was the first to spot it, and she saw it as soon as we stepped from the bus. At the bottom men and women with various weapons stood with bowed heads against the ruins of battle while others fired a volley into the folds of a banner strung up with barbed wire and printed all over with shields and crests. Above all this a golden youth towered, her gaze flung backwards over her shoulder, her right arm raised and beckoning to the dark silhouettes of the marchers who followed her – Opportunity! Culture! their placards promised, Houses! Jobs! Education for All!

Brandon Originals

Chet Raymo: *In the Falcon's Claw*

In 998, two years before what many believe will be the year of the Apocalypse, the abbot of the abandoned island monastery of Skellig Michael is called to account for heresy.

'*In the Falcon's Claw* is a novel of never-ending pleasure... superbly innovative. It is a work of rare and irreverent intelligence.' *Le Figaro Litteraire*

'A metaphysical thriller comparable to Umberto Eco's *In the Name of the Rose*, but more poetic, more moving and more sensual.' *Lire*

ISBN 0 86322 204 8; £6.95

Patrick Quigley: *Borderland*

A remarkably accomplished novel which explores the reality of living in a divided community, the borderland between the north and south of Ireland.

'A debut of remarkable assurance, polish and control.' *The Times*

'This book impressed me more than any other book I read in the first six months of 1994... it must surely be in line for an award.' *Irish World*

ISBN 0 86322 179 3; £6.95

Sean Rooney: Early Many a Morning
A gritty portrayal of working-class Belfast, for twenty-five years the battleground of an undeclared war.

'One of the most striking aspects of the book and its cold, hard narrative, is the absence of any distorting comment on the action. The story is painfully bare and unadorned... On a very personal level, the novel shows the effects that violence can have on a community.' *The Irish Post*

'The really gripping aspect of this novel is its unequivocal insider's view of... "The Troubles". Some moments in the narrative are particularly outstanding.' *Weekend*

'Impressive.' *Irish Press*

ISBN 0 86322 181 5; £6.95

Kathleen O'Farrell: The Fiddler of Kilbroney
Historical figures come alive in this meticulously crafted novel set in the 1790s, a decade which saw the birth of republicanism in Ireland.

'With her second novel... Kathleen O'Farrell secures for herself the niche she began to carve out with *Kilbroney*, as the chronicler of life in Ireland in the mid-18th century.' *Newry Reporter*

ISBN 0 86322 177 7; £7.95

Michael Dickinson: The Lost Testament of Judas Iscariot
Judas did not hang himself but went into hiding, from which he wrote a letter to Peter, giving his own account of the events which led to him being branded a traitor.

'Highly readable… a brave book… Dickinson's Judas is not the stereotyped money-grabbing traitor who sold Jesus out for a few shekels.' *Birmingham Post*

'Elegant Prose.' *Irish Press*

ISBN 0 86322 178 5; £6.95

The Alphabet Garden

A specially commissioned collection of short stories from twelve countries, which celebrates the different voices, styles and languages of young European writers.

'The stories are of a consistently high standard and display acrobatic imaginative feats couched in fresh styles.' *The Sunday Times*

ISBN 0 86322 189 0; £6.95

Robert Welch: The Kilcolman Notebook

In his study at Kilcolman Castle, Edmund Spenser sits writing of his relationships with Walter Raleigh and Queen Elizabeth, between Ireland and England. It is a story told in dreams, dreams of a strange complicity, a mutual exchange between aggressor and victim.

'There is so much good stuff I'm not sure where to begin… but if you have any interest in writing that is different and challenging you should check it out immediately.' *Books Ireland*

'Fairly crackles with intensity.' *Irish Press*

ISBN 0 86322 180 7; £6.95